P9-DNU-011

"Jessica?"

She cringed at the sound of her name. One of the Big Mesa players broke away from the pack and jogged toward her. *What?* Jessica thought. *The rumors have spread to Big Mesa now?*

When he reached her, he pulled off his helmet, removed his mouthpiece, and smiled.

Jessica blinked. "Jeremy?"

His eyes shimmered with laughter. "He's taking the day off. I'm Justin, the evil twin."

"I can't believe you're here!" she exclaimed, her heart pounding. "You play football?"

Jeremy looked down at his uniform. "Apparently," he said. They both laughed. "And you cheer."

"Every now and then," she said, grinning uncontrollably. It was so nice to see a friendly face in these halls. Her mood jumped from morose to giddy in about five seconds.

Then some movement behind Jeremy caught her eye. Melissa, Lila, and most of the squad were filing into the school. Lila spotted Jessica instantly and nudged Cherie.

Jessica froze as Cherie whispered to Melissa. Jeremy was about to discover exactly what the world thought of her.

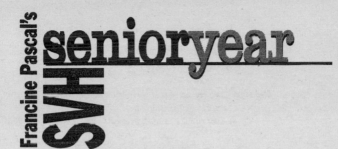

Francine Pascal's SVH senioryear

I've Got a Secret

CREATED BY
FRANCINE PASCAL

BANTAM BOOKS
NEW YORK • TORONTO • LONDON • SYDNEY • AUCKLAND

RL 6, age 12 and up

I'VE GOT A SECRET

A Bantam Book / May 1999

Sweet Valley High® is a registered trademark of Francine Pascal.
Conceived by Francine Pascal.
Cover photography by Michael Segal.

All rights reserved.
Copyright © 1999 by Francine Pascal.
Cover art copyright © 1999 by 17th Street Productions,
a division of Daniel Weiss Associates, Inc.
No part of this book may be reproduced or transmitted
in any form or by any means, electronic or mechanical,
including photocopying, recording, or by any information
storage and retrieval system, without permission in
writing from the publisher.
For information address: Bantam Books.

Produced by 17th Street Productions,
a division of Daniel Weiss Associates, Inc.
33 West 17th Street
New York, NY 10011.

If you purchased this book without a cover you should be aware
that this book is stolen property. It was reported as "unsold and
destroyed" to the publisher and neither the author nor the publisher
has received any payment for this "stripped book."

ISBN: 0-553-49278-0

Published simultaneously in the United States and Canada

Bantam Books are published by Bantam Books, a division of Random
House, Inc. Its trademark, consisting of the words "Bantam Books" and
the portrayal of a rooster, is Registered in U.S. Patent and Trademark
Office and in other countries. Marca Registrada. Bantam Books, 1540
Broadway, New York, New York 10036.

PRINTED IN THE UNITED STATES OF AMERICA

OPM   0 9 8 7 6 5 4 3 2 1

To Susan Johansson

Elizabeth Wakefield

When did everything get so complicated? One minute I was living with my family, sharing a bathroom with my fun-loving sister, hanging out with Maria and Enid, and involved in a serious, loving relationship with Todd.

Now I'm living with people I barely know. The authority figure in the house, Mrs. Sandborn, is out almost all the time. I've got this little-sister-type girl looking up to me when I don't feel worthy of being looked up to. I'm sharing a bathroom with a guy I can't stop obsessing about—a guy who just broke Maria's heart, by the way. I haven't even talked to Enid in over a week, and my sister has become a mood-swinging recluse.

And the weirdest part about the whole thing is, I feel like I've just been watching it all happen. Like I'm unable to take an active part in anything because my brain is always somewhere other than where it should be.

I have to do something. I have to take back my life.

Jessica Wakefield

Tia was the only person who still treated me like a human being. She asked me how I was doing and cared when I didn't show up for practice. I was beginning to think she was my only friend.

But then she lied to me. She gave me the wrong information about the pep rally and I missed it. And now I'll probably get thrown off the squad. She is the most fake, manipulative person I've ever known. All this time she was on Melissa's side.

And Elizabeth is friends with her.

My own sister. I really thought she'd be different from everybody else.

CHAPTER 1
Fair Is a Relative Term

"I think you know why I called you in here today, Jessica."

Jessica Wakefield stared directly at Coach Laufeld's nose, unable to meet the woman's eye. She had to play this right or get booted from the cheerleading squad. It was Monday afternoon. The week had just begun, and already she was hanging on by a thread.

"Because I missed the pep rally," Jessica stated. She made the mistake of looking up at her coach's eyes and saw the concerned yet stern expression there. Jessica shifted in her seat and focused on the Don't Drink and Drive poster on the wall behind Laufeld's head. She was feeling caged in. The athletic office was tiny, and the walls were covered with fake wood paneling. Jessica had no idea how the coaches and gym teachers spent so much time in here without getting claustrophobic.

"Not only did you miss the pep rally, but you didn't even call and let me know you wouldn't be

1

there," Coach said, leaning back in her creaking, wood-and-vinyl chair.

Jessica nervously pushed her blond hair behind her ears and opened her mouth to regurgitate her rehearsed I-had-a-stomach-flu response, but the coach cut her off.

"If one of your teammates hadn't told me you were sick, I would have had the police out looking for you."

Jessica's eyebrows popped up. "What?"

Coach Laufeld laughed. "I know it sounds extreme, but you've never missed an event," she said. "I thought you might have been in an accident or something."

Jessica could hardly process what her coach was saying. She was too busy wondering who on the squad had made up an excuse for her. All nine of them hated her. They had set her up with the wrong information so that she'd miss the rally. Why would they then provide a good excuse for her? It didn't make sense.

"I'm glad to see you're feeling better." Coach Laufeld placed her elbows on her desk and leaned forward. Her tightly curled brown hair was so long, it grazed the surface of the desk.

"Much better," Jessica said with a smile. Was she really going to get out of this? "Can I go to practice now?" She started to get up from the uncomfortable metal chair.

"Hold on a second, Wakefield."

Uh-oh. She slammed back into her seat and turned what she hoped was a pity-me expression on her coach.

"Is there anything you want to talk to me about?" Laufeld asked, her gaze focused squarely on Jessica's face. "Anything going on among the squad members?"

Jessica's heart was pounding uncomfortably, and she felt her cheeks go red. How much did Laufeld know? Or was she just following a hunch? Jessica slumped slightly in her chair and made an effort to sit up straight. She couldn't tell on her teammates. Then she'd *really* be fried.

"No, Coach," Jessica said with a completely straight face—she hoped. "Not that I can think of."

Coach Laufeld narrowed her eyes for a moment, but then she just leaned back in her chair and sighed.

"Okay, Jessica. I know I don't have to tell you this, but I'm going to anyway." She took a deep breath. "If this happens again, there are going to be serious consequences."

"Don't worry," Jessica said. "It's not going to happen again." *Not if I stop trusting people and learn to watch my back.*

"Okay. Go change your clothes and get warmed up." Coach Laufeld managed a pinched smile as she dismissed Jessica. "And Wakefield, you can always come to me if you want to talk."

"Thanks, Coach," Jessica said. She practically floated into the locker room. After she'd dreaded the encounter all weekend, that little meeting had been a cakewalk.

"Maybe my luck is changing," Jessica said under her breath.

The locker room was already deserted, which was just the way Jessica liked it lately. She grabbed her duffel bag and started to change. But as she tied the laces on her red-and-white cheerleading sneakers, all she could think about was who might have bailed her out. Maybe when she joined the squad in the gym, she'd be able to read the sympathy on someone's face. Jessica sighed as she tossed her things inside a locker. Whoever had made up her excuse, it was just nice to know that she had at least one friend on the squad.

Melissa Fox was having a hard time controlling the psychotic butterflies in her stomach. She smoothed down the front of her new, red SVH T-shirt and pulled her long, brown hair back over her shoulders.

Today was the day. Coach Laufeld had said she was going to pick a captain after the pep rally.

"Do you think she'll tell us before practice or after?" Gina Cho asked.

"She has to do it before," Melissa said, staring at the door to the athletic office and willing Laufeld to walk through it. "Waiting until later would be undue torture."

"Whatever, Liss," Cherie Reese said, pulling the band out of her ponytail. She bent at the waist and flipped down her long, red curls. "You know it's you. Jessica didn't even show up for the pep rally."

"You made sure of that," Gina said with a laugh.

Melissa couldn't believe Gina had just said that out loud. She glared at her friend until she blushed.

"What?" Gina said. "Everyone knows."

Melissa looked pointedly toward the front of the room, where Annie Whitman and Jade Wu were stretching out with Tia Ramirez. "Not everyone," she said.

Gina shrugged. "They can't hear me."

Melissa rolled her eyes and was about to retort when Cherie stood up.

"Wait! Here's Coach!" Cherie said, retying her hair.

Melissa's heart was in her mouth. Coach Laufeld walked across the gym, holding her clipboard against her chest. Jessica was walking right next to her, and she wasn't staring at the floor like she usually did. Melissa didn't know what to make

5

of that. Had Laufeld named Jessica captain? Was that what they were talking about in the athletic office?

"You don't think—"

"No way," Cherie said. "You can't miss a pep rally and be made captain."

Melissa's stomach turned. Just knowing Cherie had interpreted the situation the same way made her doubly nervous.

"That would be total favoritism," Gina put in.

"I'd like everyone's attention," Coach Laufeld said when she reached the front of the gym. Her voice echoed across the huge room. Melissa clasped her sweaty hands behind her back. "Have a seat."

The squad members dropped to the floor, and Melissa followed but kept her gaze focused on the coach. Laufeld's eyes roamed the room, and Melissa saw them rest momentarily on herself. Was that a good sign?

"I know you're all expecting me to announce a captain today—"

Melissa closed her eyes and crossed her fingers.

"But I'm not ready to make that decision just yet."

What? Melissa could barely contain herself from screeching the word aloud. She looked at Cherie, whose confused expression probably mirrored her own. *Only I'm about ten shades paler,*

Melissa thought, having felt the blood rush from her face. The squad had been working long enough without a leader. It just made practices more disorganized than they had to be.

"I just feel that I don't know the new girls well enough yet to make an informed decision, and it's important that the squad leader be the right person for the job. I promise you I'll make an announcement before the game on Saturday," Laufeld said.

"This is insane," Cherie whispered. "What else does she want to see?" Gina shrugged.

"Who wants to lead drills?" Coach Laufeld asked.

Melissa's arm shot up, and the coach motioned for her to come forward.

As she jogged to the front of the room, Melissa made a mental checklist of all the things she'd done for the squad so far.

She'd let everyone use her house to paint banners for the rally, she'd planned where and when they would meet beforehand, and they'd all allowed her to call the cheers.

She was obviously the squad's choice for captain—except for maybe one member. Melissa took her place in front of the squad and glanced at Jessica quickly, then smiled at Coach Laufeld. Now she just had one more person to convince.

*   *   *

Jeremy Aames squinted at the wall clock as he pushed open the door of House of Java. He'd just picked up his sisters from school and dropped them back home. Now he was fifteen minutes late for work. He'd never been late before, and it was making him tense.

"Hey, Liz," he said, rushing behind the counter as he pulled his apron out of his blue backpack. One of his coworkers, Elizabeth Wakefield, was sitting on a stool, sipping a latte.

"Hi, Jeremy." She looked up, and her blue-green eyes widened just slightly. "What's the matter?" she asked. "You look stressed."

"I'm late." Jeremy dropped his bag and tied on the apron. As he pushed his fingers through his short, black hair, he smiled at Suzanne, the other worker behind the counter. "Sorry, Suz."

"No problem," she said, her eyes crinkling as she smiled. "Elizabeth's an easy customer."

Jeremy glanced around the cozy coffee shop and sighed with relief. The place was practically empty. There was a couple cuddled into one of the huge, red velvet chairs and one older guy sitting at a table by the window. Other than that, there was just Elizabeth.

"So what are you doing here on your day off?" Jeremy asked, grabbing a rag from the sink and wiping down the counter. "Shouldn't you be doing day-off-type things?"

Elizabeth smiled. "I'm just wasting time. I have to go back to school and get my sister when she's done with practice."

"Oh." Jeremy mock-frowned. "So you're not here for the sparkling conversation?"

"You wish," Elizabeth joked. "Actually, I'd better go," she said as she threw a couple of dollars on the counter. She stuffed her notebook into her backpack and was just sliding off her stool when Jeremy's manager, Ally Scott, pushed open the door that led to the back room.

"Jeremy!" she exclaimed. "Can I see you back here for a minute?"

Elizabeth shot a wary look at Jeremy, and he felt his stomach jump. Was he in trouble for being late?

He managed to smile at Elizabeth. "See ya."

"Good luck," Elizabeth replied.

Jeremy dropped the rag and followed Ally's petite form into the all-purpose back room. It served as the break area, the storage closet, and a makeshift office for Ally. The owner, Mrs. Scott, who was also Ally's mother, had an actual office behind a closed door at the end of the room. Jeremy dropped into the green plastic chair next to Ally's desk.

"Listen, Al," he began. "I'm really sorry I—"

"Do you realize what today is?" Ally pulled her chair out and sat down, facing Jeremy.

He racked his brain. "Um . . . no."

"It's your anniversary," Ally said. "You've been working here for one year today."

"Really?" Jeremy asked, thinking back. He couldn't believe he'd held one job for that long. House of Java was like a revolving door for high-school employees. People usually only stayed around long enough to stash a respectable amount of party money. "So do I win a prize or something?" Jeremy joked.

"Well, sort of," Ally said as she straightened some papers on her desk. She pulled out an envelope and handed it to Jeremy.

He turned it over in his hands. It was thin and brown—like a standard HOJ paycheck envelope. "What is it?"

"Just open it," Ally ordered, pulling her strawberry-blond hair behind her shoulders.

Jeremy complied. He removed his paycheck for the previous week and looked at the amount. Then he blinked and looked again. The number was a lot bigger than it usually was.

"A raise?" Jeremy asked. His heart was pounding. He could *so* use this money.

"A raise," Ally confirmed, smiling. "You're getting a dollar-fifty more an hour as of that paycheck."

Jeremy leaned forward and hugged her, and Ally laughed in surprise. "God, Jeremy. You're still practically slave labor!" she said, patting him on the back.

"Maybe," Jeremy said, leaning back. "But you have no idea what this means to me."

"Hey." Ally slapped his knee. "It means a lot to me too. That's the first time anyone has stuck around long enough for me to give them a raise."

"Thanks, Ally."

"Thank *you*," Ally said. She stood up from her desk. "Just don't mention it around Mom."

Jeremy stood too, carefully folding the check and sliding it into the back pocket of his jeans. "She doesn't know?" he asked. Mrs. Scott was a notorious penny-pincher. She even counted sugar packets and was always accusing Elizabeth of hiding them. Of course, Elizabeth *did* hide them just to irritate Mrs. Scott, but Jeremy would never tell.

"Oh, she knows. She's just not very happy about it," Ally said. "She knew we had to do it, though."

"Well, thanks again," Jeremy said. "I'm going to go start earning my raise."

Back behind the counter, Jeremy couldn't stop grinning. After work, he was going to go right home and tell his mom she had the night off from cooking. Then he was going to call The Golden Pond and order Chinese food for his whole family. Jeremy knew he'd probably feel guilty tomorrow about spending the cash, but he didn't care. It had

been a long time since he had anything to cele-
brate.

Elizabeth Wakefield checked her watch.
Cheerleading practice would be over any minute.
She'd called her mother and offered to pick Jessica
up at school so that she could get a moment alone
with her sister. They had been playing hide-and-
seek all day. Unfortunately, Elizabeth was always
the seeker.

"Hey, Liz! What're you doing here?"

Tia Ramirez was the first person out the door,
followed by a crowd of gabbing girls who immediately took off toward the parking lot. Elizabeth
saw Lila and Cherie bringing up the rear, and they
seemed to be engaged in some heated debate.
Elizabeth wondered if they were arguing over the
latest nail polish or the latest hair gel.

"I'm picking up Jessica," Elizabeth said, pulling
at a stray thread hanging from the hem of her
white T-shirt. "I'm going to try to anyway. She
hasn't talked to me all day."

Tia dropped her gym bag on the ground in
front of her. She pulled her long, dark brown hair
off her shoulders and quickly twisted it into a bun.
"I'm so sorry about this."

"It's not your fault," Elizabeth said, watching
the door. "You didn't do anything."

"Maybe I should stick around and talk to her

12

with you," Tia suggested. "I could explain what happened."

Elizabeth smiled. "Sounds like a plan. I'd love to hear the whole story too. Now all we have to do is figure out how to keep her from bolting."

Jessica walked through the door and froze, her eyes darting from Elizabeth to Tia and back again. "Ambush time?" she asked.

"It's not an ambush, Jess," Elizabeth said. She knew from experience that she had to say the important stuff right away before Jessica cut her off and heard nothing. "Tia didn't set you up—they set *her* up."

Jessica hesitated, shifting her red gym bag on her shoulder. "What do you mean?"

Tia took a deep breath. "Cherie called me and told me about the change of plans," Tia explained. "She said Lila was going to tell you because you lived together, but then she told Lila you already knew. She just lied to everybody. As far as I know, when I told you we were going to meet at Melissa's, that was still the plan."

Jessica's shoulders sagged as if the air had been drained out of her.

"Are you okay?" Elizabeth asked. She stepped forward and took Jessica's bags from her. She'd never seen her sister look so broken. Elizabeth could kill Cherie Reese.

"I should have known." Jessica plopped down

on the top step. "I just can't believe Cherie," she said with tears in her voice. "What is wrong with that girl? What did I ever do to her?" She looked up at Elizabeth, her bright blue-green eyes rimmed with red.

To Elizabeth's surprise, Tia sat down next to Jessica on the concrete and wrapped an arm around her back. She had no idea Tia felt so close to her sister. "I don't know why she's doing this," Tia said, "but she's going to get hers."

"What do you mean?" Elizabeth and Jessica asked in unison.

Tia looked at Elizabeth, her hand still resting on Jessica's shoulder. "I mean this whole thing has got to stop. I just feel bad that I haven't said anything sooner."

Jessica stood up abruptly, pulling down on her gray cotton shorts. "This isn't your problem, Tia," Jessica said. "I'm sorry I blamed you, but you shouldn't put yourself in the middle."

"I'm not putting myself in the middle," Tia said. She stood up and grabbed her bag. "Cherie put me in the middle, and I'm sure Melissa had something to do with it. I don't appreciate being used."

Elizabeth had only known Tia for a short while, and she'd always been hyper and cheerful. This fighting side was impressive. "What're you going to do?" Elizabeth asked.

Tia grinned, put an arm around each of the twins, and started for the parking lot. "I think it's time for a good, old-fashioned shoot-out, don't you?"

Elizabeth shot Jessica a look and could tell her sister was as clueless as she was. But whatever Tia was planning, the mischievous glint in her eyes made Jessica smile.

And that was enough for Elizabeth.

Jeremy Aames

Application Essay #1
Write about one major event that has changed your
life significantly and explain why.

I should probably say it was studying
about the life of Abraham Lincoln, or
volunteering at a homeless shelter after
the earthquake, or the time I went hiking
in Sequoia National Park. But I'd be
lying if I did. Then again, my whole life
became a lie last year when my father
lost his job. And filling out this
application is probably a big waste of
time because it doesn't look like I'll even
be able to afford college next year.

I don't know what's worse, the fact
that we're falling apart here, along with
the house, or that we have to pretend
everything is fine. I see my dad every
morning at the kitchen table, drinking
black coffee, reading The Wall Street
Journal. Then he goes into his study and

surfs the Internet all day while the bills pile up and the water heater keeps shorting out the fuse box.

My sisters are too little to know what's going on, and my mom is stuck in denial. So it's up to me. My job at House of Java started out as a way to earn gas money. Now it's buying groceries and paying bills. I thought of quitting school so I could work full-time, but it would've blown our cover as the perfectly normal American family. So I keep lying to everyone: my friends, my sisters, the people I work with at HOJ. . . .

So I guess that's the major event that changed my life—the day my father was canned and I learned to lie.

CHAPTER
Alone in the Crowd
2

"Thank you, Debbie," Jeremy said as he pulled his father's vintage Mercedes into Big Mesa High's student parking lot Tuesday morning. He'd nicknamed the old car Debbie when he'd started driving it the year before, and it hadn't let him down since. This morning was no exception.

"You talkin' to your car again, man?"

Jeremy nearly jumped out of his skin. Alex Harris was leaning on the passenger-side window. His blue oxford shirt was freshly pressed as usual, and his wide grin proudly displayed the effects of thousands of dollars' worth of orthodontics.

"Yeah, man," Jeremy said, climbing out of the car. He ran his hands through his hair and smiled. "She got me here on fumes."

"There's at least three gas stations between here and your house. Why didn't you stop?" Alex asked. Jeremy reached into the backseat for his book bag and his blue-and-gold varsity jacket. *Because my wallet's below empty, just like my gas tank,* he thought.

He pulled on his jacket, shouldered his bag, and slammed the car door. "Blew all my cash on CDs," he said, casually twirling his keys on his finger. "Dad keeps telling me I need to learn to budget."

"Yeah, right," Alex said, slapping Jeremy on the back with a laugh. Jeremy shook his head as they started across the parking lot. Alex probably didn't know the meaning of the word *budget*.

Jeremy felt the blood start to rise in his face and told himself to calm down. Being jealous of his friends wouldn't change the fact that he had to pay a plumber to fix the leaky water heater—the heater that should've been replaced months ago but wasn't because a new water heater was an out-of-the-question luxury these days. Why did he have to live in the richest town in southern California?

"Hey, guys!"

Jeremy looked up to find his best friend, Trent Maynor, standing with a crowd a few parking spaces away. Jeremy smiled. Trent was wearing his standard uniform of a white, V-neck T-shirt and blue jeans. He said the shirt showed off his deep ebony skin and perfect quarterback body. The guy was not short on confidence.

"You have to see this!" Trent called.

Jeremy looked toward the sprawling school building, stalling. A mixed crowd of guys meant one of two things. Either there was a fight going on, or someone had just been given a hot new car. There was no yelling and flailing, so Jeremy figured it was the latter, and he wasn't interested in fawning over some shiny automobile.

"C'mon, man," Alex said, jogging toward the group.

Jeremy walked over and caught a glimpse of the car through the crowd. It was a silver BMW Z3, and it had come to school with Sarah Isaacs.

Trent stroked the chrome trim and turned to Jeremy. "Not bad, huh?"

"It's great," he replied automatically.

"It's my dad's," Sarah explained. "My Celica's in the shop because some belt or other busted yesterday afternoon."

"This is my dream vehicle," Alex said, petting the hood as if it were made of mink. "Can I drive it?"

Sarah blushed. "I don't know if—"

"How fast does it go?" Jeremy asked, trying to save Sarah from having to deal with Alex.

"Not over the speed limit," Sarah said.

The crowd groaned as if they'd all been mortally wounded. "What a waste!"

"Hey, I value my life!" Sarah protested. "And my dad would *kill* me if I got a speeding ticket in this car."

"What if *I* got a speeding ticket in this car?" Alex asked, tossing his arm around her shoulders. Everyone laughed.

Some of the guys began bugging Sarah for a ride home that day, but of course only one of them could be accommodated in the two seater, so it was a fight to the finish. Sarah giggled, visibly flattered by all the attention.

"Pathetic, isn't it?" Trent said, joining Jeremy on the periphery.

"I hope she realizes what's up," Jeremy said.

"I know, man," Trent said. "That girl was never that popular when she was driving a Toyota."

Jeremy started walking toward the school, and Trent fell into step with him.

"Where do they get off?" Jeremy asked. "She's a nice girl. They shouldn't treat her that way over a car. They're so freakin' shallow."

Trent held open the school door. "Good one, Mr. I-drive-a-Mercedes-convertible."

"You know that's my dad's," Jeremy said, dodging a girl who was squatting in front of her locker.

"Yeah, but still—"

"Still nothing," Jeremy spat. "I wasn't handed the keys to a brand-new ride when I turned seventeen like everyone else."

Trent stopped in his tracks. "What's your problem?" he asked.

Jeremy took a deep breath. Trent knew Jeremy's dad had hit rough times, but he had no idea how bad things were. He didn't know that Jeremy had become one of those people the residents of Big

Mesa never talked about. One of those people who had to worry about how to pay for his next meal.

"I'm sorry, man," Jeremy said. "Just a little stressed, I guess."

"That's cool," Trent said, patting Jeremy's shoulder. "You good?"

"Yeah, I'm good."

"All right, then." Trent smiled. "I'll catch you in the caf." He took off down the hall.

Jeremy sighed and headed for his own homeroom. He really hoped his dad would find work soon, and not just because he was tired or stressed. And definitely not because he wanted a new car.

Jeremy was just getting tired of lying to his friends.

Will Simmons paid for his lunch on Tuesday afternoon and turned reluctantly toward his friends' table near the windows. Everyone was assembled. Melissa and her girlfriends were already in full gossip mode, and the guys were shoving enough food in their mouths to feed a small country. Will sighed and walked along the wall toward the table. *Just don't let them be talking about Jessica,* he thought.

"She'll probably tell us at practice one day this week," Cherie said as Melissa pulled out a chair for Will.

"Who'll tell you what?" Will asked, putting down his tray.

"Coach Laufeld said she'd announce the captain before the game on Saturday," Gina explained. "We're just trying to figure out if she meant sometime this week or right *before* the game."

Will popped open his soda can and glanced at Melissa. Jessica was her main competition for the captainship, so this conversation could turn ugly unless it was steered in the right direction.

"Who cares?" Will said. "You know you've got it in the bag." He leaned over and kissed Melissa on the cheek. "No offense to you guys," he told her friends.

Melissa smiled, but Will saw her knock the wooden underside of the table. He shook his head. Her little superstitions were too funny. But she took them very seriously, so he knew better than to say anything.

"Of course Melissa's going to be captain. We just think it should be official by now," Gina said. "I mean, I get the whole waiting-to-see-us-work-together thing, but she saw us all last week."

"Maybe she just doesn't think she knows us well enough," Melissa said. She pushed her salad around with her plastic fork and finally speared a semired tomato slice. "I guess I can see her point."

"I wish Coach Riley had done the same thing," Will said, leaning his elbows on the table. "After

Ken Matthews quit the team, he never even bothered to name a new captain. You need to have someone in charge, you know?"

"Definitely," Melissa said, smiling. Will knew Melissa was just as sure as he was that she was going to get the position. He was happy for her, and he was also happy that Jessica-bashing seemed to be over. If this little crowd of girls could get through an entire conversation about cheerleading without mentioning Jessica, well, that was a good sign.

Maybe she's finally getting over it, Will thought as the girls started discussing which uniforms to wear to the first game. Soon he might even be able to talk to Jessica without looking over his shoulder. And then he would have time to apologize.

Will smiled as he dug into his lunch. His shoulder muscles started to unknot for the first time in weeks.

"Hey, who's this?" Jessica asked, pointing to a picture taped to the inside of Tia's locker on Tuesday afternoon. There was a beautiful African American guy with his arms wrapped around a grinning Tia from behind.

"That's my sweetie, Angel," Tia said.

"He's gorgeous," Jessica commented.

"No kidding," Tia said. She quickly kissed her

24

finger and touched the photo, then smiled at Jessica. "Don't get any ideas."

Jessica's eyes dropped to the ground.

"Oh, Jess!" Tia said. "I'm just kidding. I know you wouldn't—"

Jessica looked up and managed a wry smile. "I know you didn't mean anything," she said.

"I'm just going to take my foot out of my mouth. Give me a second," Tia said. She rummaged through the bottom of her locker and pulled out a notebook. "Okay. Are you ready?" Tia asked, stuffing the notebook into her bag. Jessica's heart flopped just from Tia's tone.

"Ready for what?" she asked as Tia slammed her locker door.

"For Melissa," Tia said. She swung her backpack onto one shoulder and picked up her duffel bag from the floor. "I'm going to have a little chat with her before practice."

"A little chat," Jessica repeated. She followed Tia down the hall, heading for the gym. When Tia had mentioned a shoot-out yesterday, Jessica had had no idea that she was supposed to be involved as well. She had a feeling that if she said one word to Melissa, no matter what it was about, the conversation would immediately return to Jessica's "slut" status. It was one of Melissa and her friends' favorite lies to perpetuate.

"What're you going to say to her?" Jessica asked

as she and Tia rounded the corner into the small lobby outside the gym.

They both stopped. Will Simmons and Melissa were in the center of a little crowd hanging out in front of the locker rooms. Cherie Reese, Gina Cho, and Matt Wells all looked over.

"I don't know, but we're about to find out," Tia said. Jessica stood frozen in place as Tia strolled over to the group. Conversation gradually faded away as tension became the mood of the moment. Jessica considered hiding in the locker room.

"Melissa, can I talk to you for a minute?" Tia asked.

Melissa looked at Will, who shrugged. "What's up?" Melissa asked.

"Maybe we should go outside," Tia suggested, angling toward the gym-lobby entrance.

"Why?" Melissa asked, visibly tensing.

"What's going on?" Will asked.

Tia took a deep breath and glanced at Jessica, who shook her head slightly. She wasn't going over there. Part of her even wished Tia would just give it up. This whole scene had a very Alamo air about it.

"I just don't think that Melissa wants everyone to hear what I have to say," Tia said.

"I'm kinda curious about it," Matt said, obviously loving the tension. *What an idiot,* Jessica thought.

Melissa's grip on her books tightened, and she moved an inch closer to Will. Jessica saw Will place his hand on Melissa's shoulder protectively. He was acting like a bodyguard. A thick silence hung in the air.

"Fine, here it is," Tia said finally. "I really don't appreciate the fact that you and your friends used me to make Jessica miss the pep rally." She shot Cherie a scathing look. "I don't like being lied to, and I think what you did to Jessica sucks."

Will quickly looked at Jessica. She glanced away a second after noticing the scared-rabbit look in his eyes.

"I don't know what you're talking about," Melissa said.

Tia laughed. "I'm talking about the fact that you conveniently disinvited everyone from coming to your house before the pep rally and Jessica was the only one who wasn't told."

"So how exactly were you lied to?" Cherie piped up.

"When you told me Lila informed Jessica about the change of plans," Tia said. "I volunteered to tell Jessica, and you said it was already taken care of."

Melissa smiled and stood up a little straighter. "It's not our fault if Lila forgot to talk to Jessica," she said.

"Somehow I have a feeling that it is," Tia

responded. She stepped closer to Melissa, completely ignoring the fact that Will was hovering over them. Matt was grinning as if he was ready for a catfight. "I know about a lot of things you've done, Melissa," Tia said. "I'm not stupid. And I bet Coach Laufeld would be very interested in hearing about everything you've been up to since school started."

Melissa blinked. For a second Jessica thought Tia had her. They all knew that if Tia told Laufeld what happened at the pep rally, Melissa and Cherie could both be chucked off the squad. Jessica held her breath. Then Melissa's lower lip started to tremble.

"How can you threaten me, Tia?" Melissa's voice broke. "I thought you were my friend."

Tia stepped back again, looking amused. "Don't even go there, Melissa. I'm not going to say anything . . . yet."

"I didn't even *do* anything," Melissa said, looking at Will. He was staring out the glass doors. She glanced at Cherie and Gina.

"Whatever," Tia said. "Just don't do anything *else.*"

"Are you done yet?" Cherie asked, staring Tia down.

"*I* am," Melissa said. She whirled around and pulled open the door to the girls' locker room. Will took a step back to let her go as Cherie and Gina scrambled to follow her.

"Thanks for the show, Tia," Matt said with a laugh. He turned to walk into the guys' locker room but stopped to glance at Will. "You comin', man?"

Will stooped and picked his gym bag up off the floor. He looked at Jessica again, his blue-gray eyes full of sorrow. Jessica didn't know if he felt bad for his girlfriend, for her, or for himself.

Tia walked over and leaned against the wall next to Jessica. "That went well," she muttered.

"I can't believe she actually denied everything," Jessica said, her heart pounding from the excitement of the confrontation. "Is she delusional?"

"Just a pathological liar, mostly," Tia said.

"And now I'm supposed to go in there?" Jessica asked, gesturing limply at the locker room.

Tia slung her arm around Jessica's shoulders. "Think of it this way," she said. "At least they probably want to kill me now instead of you."

Jessica smiled weakly. "Thanks, Tia."

"Don't mention it."

melissa Fox

I don't understand Tia. I've known her forever. maybe we haven't really been friends since fourth grade, when everyone was still friends with everyone, but I never thought of her as a back stabber. Or a drama queen. She's never been, or seemed to want to be, the center of attention.

I guess Jessica Wakefield is rubbing off on her.

Too Much Baggage

Will Simmons rubbed a towel against the back of his wet head as he walked out of the locker room after practice on Tuesday afternoon. A cool breeze ruffled his hair, slightly soothing his fried nerves. He'd showered and rushed out before anyone else had even finished stripping off their uniforms. After Tia's little proclamation and a grueling practice, all Will wanted to do was get home and kick back in front of some bad reruns.

"Oh, man," he muttered. Melissa was across the parking lot, leaning against his driver's-side door with her bags on the ground next to her. She was supposed to get a ride from Cherie today, but she obviously wanted to talk to him instead. There was a time when the sight of her waiting for him like that would have excited him. It used to make him feel special and loved. Now he just felt trapped.

Melissa looked up as Will approached. As he leaned over to casually kiss her cheek, she wrapped both arms around his neck and squeezed.

31

"You're here," Melissa said into his chest.

"Yeah, I'm here," he responded, patting her on the back. He popped open the door of his blue Chevy Blazer and threw his bag in the backseat. Melissa was watching his every move—he could feel it. And he knew she was wondering why he hadn't really returned the hug. He slung the towel over his shoulder. "What's up?"

He knew exactly what she was going to say.

"I can't believe Tia," Melissa said, crossing her slim arms in front of her. "How could she do that to me? And in front of everyone."

"You were the one who turned down the offer to go outside," Will reminded her. "And she was just sticking up for herself."

Melissa's eyes widened. "I didn't do any of the things she said, Will. I—"

"Yeah, you did, Liss," Will said. There was a bite in his voice that surprised even him.

"You don't believe me?" Melissa asked. Her eyes started to fill, and Will felt his resolve weaken, but he told himself to toughen up. This time he wasn't going to just keep his mouth shut.

"I heard you, Melissa," he said, stuffing his hands in the pockets of his khakis. Melissa's brow knitted.

"Heard me what?" she asked.

"Tell Cherie what to do—that she should call everyone except Jessica and tell them to meet at the gym instead of your house."

Melissa turned her profile to him and leaned back against the car. "What, are you spying on me or something?"

"That's not the point," Will said, turning to go.

"You're just gonna leave?" Melissa asked. "What do you want me to say?"

Will sighed and looked at the ground. "Why did you do it?" he asked. "Why can't you just drop this whole anti-Jessica thing?" He shifted his weight uncomfortably. "It's not like you."

Melissa placed her hands over her face and started to sob quietly. Will's heart melted as he watched her tiny form shaking with sobs. He pushed his fists deeper into his pockets to try to keep from reaching out to her.

"Everyone hates me." Melissa sniffled. "I didn't do anything. She started all of this." She removed her hands, and her eyes were the bright green-blue they became when she cried. Tears were rolling down her face, and there were red lines running through her skin. Whether or not she deserved to be put in her place by Tia, it was obvious that Melissa was really hurting from the public humili-ation. Will reached out and pulled her to him.

"No one hates you," he said as she cried into his sweater.

"Tia does."

"Forget about Tia," Will said. "You've never cared what she thought before."

Melissa just sniffled in response.

"C'mon, it's going to be all right," Will said. He hoped he didn't sound as wooden as he felt inside. His words could have been taken from a script he'd used many times.

"No, it's not," Melissa said with a sob. "Tia's going to tell Laufeld, and she and Jessica are going to get me thrown off the squad."

Will sighed. "Tia said she wouldn't do that," he said. "So she won't." He'd known Tia Ramirez for a long time, and he knew she was true to her word.

Melissa pulled back. "I hope you're right." She wiped the back of her hands across her cheeks, then sighed deeply. "Can you just take me home?" she asked weakly, hugging herself. "I'm really tired all of a sudden."

"Sure," Will said. He picked up her bags and put them in the backseat. Melissa walked around to the other side of the truck. Will sat down, feeling as if his arms weighed about two hundred pounds each.

He didn't want to be in the car with Melissa right now. Just the thought was suffocating. She had avoided answering his questions about why she'd sabotaged Jessica. Nothing he said mattered anymore. He'd become nothing more than a shoulder to cry on, and he wasn't even sure he wanted to be that anymore.

Melissa knocked on the window, and Will

reached over to pop the lock. She climbed into the car and smiled at him wanly.

Will tried to smile back. But as he pulled out of the parking lot, one thought pressed in on his temples with aching clarity.

If this was the way their relationship was going to be, he wanted out. And sooner or later, he was going to have to tell her.

"This is a really nice place," Tia said as Elizabeth led her out to the deck at the Box Tree Café on Tuesday night. "I'm glad we decided to come here instead of going to House of Java or First and Ten. If I have one more Touchdown Turkey Burger, I'm gonna die." She looked out at the ocean, then took a peek over the railing at the cliffs below.

"I know," Elizabeth said. "And I can't even look at biscotti anymore. Working at HOJ has turned me off that stuff forever." As she sat down at a table and opened the familiar menu, she took a deep breath of the soothing ocean air. "I feel like I haven't been to the beach in years. I really needed to get out of the house."

"So living at Conner's isn't a dream existence?" Tia asked, dropping into the chair across from Elizabeth's.

Elizabeth felt her face grow warm. Tia had known Conner and his family a long time, and she didn't want to offend her friend. "No, it's fine," Elizabeth said. "I just—"

"Are you kidding? I can't imagine what it would be like living under the same roof with Conner the Uptight," Tia said. "The boy is impossible."

Elizabeth laughed, relieved. "No kidding. I feel like I have to watch every move I make around him."

"All right, so if you're here to get away, let's not talk about Sir Moody," Tia said, picking up her menu. "There have to be more interesting topics of conversation."

Elizabeth clasped her hands under the table. Suddenly she had an idea. She'd been dying to get someone's advice on her situation with Conner. And Tia knew him better than anyone. . . .

But no. She couldn't tell Tia how she really felt. The fact that Tia had been friends with Conner forever meant that her advice would come with too much baggage. What Elizabeth really needed was a nonpartisan opinion. Of course, maybe she could still get one . . . if she played her cards right.

"Can I ask your advice about something?" Elizabeth asked as Tia put her menu down.

"Is it a guy?" Tia asked, her eyes bright.

Elizabeth stopped chewing on her bottom lip. "How did you know?"

"It's always about a guy," Tia said. "Unless it's about people torturing your sister, and I think we're done with that now."

"Thanks for that, by the way," Elizabeth said. "Jessica said you were great."

"No problem. Now back to the guy." The waiter came and took their orders. When he'd gone back inside, Elizabeth leaned forward in her chair.

"Okay, I have this massive crush—"

Tia squealed. "On who?"

"You don't know him," Elizabeth lied. "He goes to another school."

"What's his name?" Tia asked, crunching on some ice from her water glass.

Elizabeth squirmed and pushed her light blond hair behind her ears. "Let's just call him 'Guy'. The problem is, Guy acts like he couldn't care less about me."

"So forget about him," Tia said, leaning back. "You deserve a guy who'll treat you like a goddess. We all do."

"I can't," Elizabeth said. "Forget about him, I mean. Trust me. I've tried."

"Really?" Tia asked.

Elizabeth rested her elbows on the white linen tablecloth. "Tia, I swear it's like I have a brain virus or something. I'm certifiable, off-the-wall, possibly dangerous."

"Well, that's a given," Tia said with a laugh. Elizabeth giggled weakly. "Can I ask you something?" Tia asked.

"Sure," Elizabeth said.

"He's totally wrong for you, right?" Tia asked, holding her hair off her face as the wind whipped it around. "Like, the complete opposite of your dream guy."

Elizabeth nodded. "Pretty much."

"He's a complete jerk, but somehow you've decided he's really sensitive and he just needs to open up to you," Tia stated.

Elizabeth stared at the single flower in the center of the table, feeling raw. "It sounds so stupid."

"It's not stupid," Tia said. She pulled her chair closer to the table. "It's totally classic. The lure of the unavailable. Everybody goes through it."

Elizabeth felt a stirring of hope. "You think that's all it is? One of those if-you-had-him-you-wouldn't-want-him things?"

"You got it," Tia said. "And I know exactly what you should do."

"What?" Elizabeth asked.

"Kiss him." Tia's brown eyes flashed mischievously.

Elizabeth's heart dropped along with her jaw. The waiter appeared and placed their dishes in front of them. Tia was smirking as she leaned back and smoothed her napkin across her lap. She started to chow down before Elizabeth had even unfrozen.

"Are you serious?" Elizabeth asked finally. Just the thought of kissing Conner put her pulse into overdrive. How could doing it help her? She'd probably suffer a heart attack if their lips ever touched.

"It's like this," Tia explained as she munched on some lettuce. "What you're feeling right now isn't love, right?" She pointed at Elizabeth with her fork.

"Right . . . ," Elizabeth said skeptically.

"It's more like an obsession. So when you kiss him, you'll realize there are no real sparks."

"I don't know, Tia—"

"You can either grab the bull by the horns and do it or wait around feeling all heartsick for months until you finally hook up with him under the mistletoe at some Christmas party and realize he's not all that." Tia paused for breath. "Do you really want to waste half your senior year wondering?"

"I guess that makes sense," Elizabeth said slowly. She stared at her untouched spaghetti. Her insides were so tied up, she couldn't even think of eating.

"Trust me," Tia said, gathering a forkful of salad. "Kissing may be fun, but only one kiss in a hundred tells you that you've found true love. Chances are, you're going to see that he's just a regular guy and your crush will instantly dissolve."

Elizabeth leaned back in her chair. It would be so great if Tia were right. Elizabeth wouldn't have to worry about Maria finding out about her feelings for Conner anymore. She wouldn't have to be nervous at his house all the time, wondering where he was and if she was going to bump into him in the bathroom or on her way to bed. But still—

"How am I supposed to do it?" Elizabeth asked. "Just walk up to him and throw my arms around him?"

"That's one approach," Tia said.

Elizabeth's stomach churned, and she pushed her plate away. There were two small obstacles to Tia's plan. Elizabeth was sure she didn't have the guts to pull it off, and Conner might die laughing in the process.

TIA RAMIREZ

ELIZABETH IS SO OBVIOUSLY IN LOVE WITH CONNER.

AND CONNER SO OBVIOUSLY NEEDS A GIRLFRIEND LIKE ELIZABETH.

I GUESS THAT DOESN'T MAKE WHAT I DID OKAY. I MEAN, MAYBE I SHOULDN'T HAVE TOLD ELIZABETH TO THROW HERSELF AT CONNER, BUT I FIGURE ONE OF TWO THINGS WILL HAPPEN.

1. CONNER WILL TELL HER HE'S NOT INTERESTED, EVEN THOUGH I KNOW HE IS, AND ELIZABETH WILL GET ON WITH HER LIFE;
   OR
2. CONNER WILL WAKE UP AND REALIZE THAT ELIZABETH IS THE

PERFECT YIN TO HIS TOTALLY
MOODY YANG AND THEY'LL LIVE
HAPPILY EVER AFTER.

STRANGER THINGS HAVE
HAPPENED.

CHAPTER 4
Invitations

Elizabeth grimaced when she saw her reflection in the locker-room mirror after gym class. Her hair was a frizzy mess, except for her bangs, which were stuck to her forehead in sweaty clumps.

"So Tia really let Melissa have it, huh?" Maria asked, tying a purple scarf around her short mop of curls. "Too bad we weren't there."

"I know. It would have been great to see Melissa's face," Elizabeth said. She took her hairbrush out of her bag and went to work on the frizz. "Did you hear all the fictional versions that are circulating?"

"Yeah, like Tia slapped Melissa and pushed her into the wall . . . that Melissa tried to choke Tia and a bunch of guys had to pull them apart," Maria said with a laugh. "The gossip mill around here is unreal!"

"Seriously. I even heard that Will threatened Tia," Elizabeth said, uncapping a lipstick.

"That wouldn't surprise me, the way he's always walking around here like he's her protector or something." Maria slammed her locker shut. "Come on, Liz. I'm starving."

"Just a minute," Elizabeth said. She pressed her lips together and checked her teeth. She still looked completely disheveled. "I guess there's nothing I can do."

"You look fine," Maria said.

"Thanks," Elizabeth responded, feeling anything but fine.

As they headed toward the cafeteria, Elizabeth tried to keep up her end of the conversation.

"So, are you totally lost in AP physics yet?" Maria asked.

"Not totally," Elizabeth answered. *Maybe I should just do it today after school,* she thought. *Grab him and kiss him.*

"I think the only class I'm acing at the moment is drama," Maria said. "Would you read over the piece I picked out for my next monologue? I'm not sure about it."

"Okay," Elizabeth said. *Oh! But I have to work tonight, and he probably won't be around right after school.*

"I still can't believe Dalton gave us a pop quiz in French," Maria lamented.

"I know," Elizabeth said. *What if he doesn't kiss me back?* she thought, completely tuning out as Maria continued talking. *What if he laughs in my face? There's no way I can do this. It doesn't even make sense.*

"So, do you think I should go for it?" Maria said.

"Well . . . um . . ." Elizabeth caught her bottom lip between her teeth. She hadn't heard what exactly Maria wanted to go for. How was she going to get out of this one?

"Be honest," Maria insisted.

Honest? Elizabeth thought. *As in admitting the truth? That would go over well. Sorry, Maria. I don't know what you're talking about. I used to have a functioning brain, and I miss it very much. But don't worry; I'm going to kiss Conner one time, and then everything will be back to normal.* Yeah, right.

Maria gave her a pointed look as she opened the cafeteria door. "You don't think I should do it, huh?"

Elizabeth lowered her eyes. "Only if it's what you really want." *I am such a fake!*

The room was noisy and crowded, but Elizabeth immediately spotted Conner. It was as if a bleep had gone off on her radar screen. He was sitting at a table with some other kids from El Carro, including Tia, which would make it perfectly okay for Elizabeth to go over and sit with them.

Of course if he dissed her in front of everyone, that might throw her kiss planning off for the rest of the day. Plus she knew Maria would never go over there.

Tia stood up and waved, inviting Elizabeth and Maria over to her table. Elizabeth waved back, smiling.

"We can sit with them if you want to," Maria said.

"That's okay," Elizabeth said quickly. "We can find another table." She knew Maria might be uncomfortable hanging around with Conner, and she didn't blame her.

Maria glanced at Conner and then squared her shoulders. "No. There's no reason to let him keep us from sitting with your friends, right? Besides, I wouldn't mind hanging out with Tia and Andy a little more . . . since you like them so much."

Elizabeth smiled. "Good," she said.

"And maybe it's time to show Conner that I'm over him," Maria said.

Elizabeth followed Maria through the maze of tables and book bags. Things were looking up. If Maria considered herself over Conner, maybe she wouldn't freak if she knew about Elizabeth's feelings. Maybe she could even talk to Maria about it.

Right, Elizabeth thought. *And maybe one day you'll outgrow your unrealistic, Little-Miss-Sunshine optimism.*

Conner's friend Evan Plummer was sitting with Andy Marsden on one side of the table, across from Tia and Conner. Maria sat down in the empty seat next to Andy. Elizabeth saw

Conner glance at Maria, then focus intently on his food. Elizabeth mentally groaned as she approached. She could either walk around the table and sit next to Tia or she could sit next to Conner, in the nearest vacant chair—the one that had Conner's bag on it.

Conner looked up, saw her, and pulled his backpack to the floor.

"Thanks," Elizabeth said, trying not to smile too brightly. It wasn't exactly an engraved invitation, but he wouldn't have done it if he didn't want her to sit there.

Elizabeth glanced at Maria, who looked like her dog just died. Luckily Evan was in a talkative mood.

"We were just talking about how Tia whipped Melissa's butt," Evan said. He grabbed Tia's hand and raised her arm up. "Winner and still champion!"

Tia giggled and pulled her arm free. "You're next if you don't stop making a big deal out of the whole thing."

Evan clutched his chest, pulling at his tie-dyed T-shirt. "I'm real scared!"

"You should be," Conner said with a small smile.

Maria glanced at him, and by the look in her eyes it was clear that she was still very much *not* over him. Elizabeth tried to concentrate on unwrapping her sandwich. If she kept thinking about all her emotional pitfalls during meals, she was never going to eat again.

"Friday night," Conner said, snapping his fingers as if he'd just remembered something important. "Guess who's opening for Silver Chair at the coliseum."

"Cosmic Thrush," Andy replied.

Conner shook his head. "They canceled. The lead singer checked into rehab."

"Again?" Tia asked. "Hasn't he already been detoxed of everything there is?"

"Making millions of dollars and having beautiful women chase you all over the country is highly stressful, Tia," Andy said dryly as he rubbed an apple against his sleeve. "Conner will explain it to you one day."

"Yeah, right," Conner said, grinning.

Elizabeth felt herself blush. She so loved his smile.

"Anyway," Conner continued, "Parallax is taking their place for the rest of the tour."

"You're kidding!" Tia said, dropping her chocolate-chip cookie on her tray. "Gavin must be so psyched."

"That's too cool, man," Evan said. He tossed his head back to get his long, black bangs out of his eyes. "You're like, one degree of separation from a rock star."

"What's Parallax?" Elizabeth asked. She hated being out of the loop.

"The lead guitarist is Conner's music teacher," Tia explained.

"Oh, wow," Elizabeth said. "Are you going to the concert?" she asked Conner.

He turned to her and smiled. Smiled. At her. Elizabeth's heart pounded loudly.

"We all are," Conner said.

Elizabeth was too stunned by the invitation to move. Luckily everyone else freaked out, so no one noticed her catatonic state.

"Free tickets and backstage passes," Conner announced.

Elizabeth finally pulled herself out of her suspended glee and glanced at Maria. Her best friend shot her a look of alarm, as if pleading with her for advice. Elizabeth shrugged. She really didn't know what to tell Maria, but Elizabeth was going to that concert.

Elizabeth's mind went into overdrive. *I'll have to find somebody to work my shift on Friday,* she thought. *A concert. In a dark coliseum, away from the daily grind, with excitement and energy in the air* . . . "Count me in."

"Me too," Maria said. She gave Elizabeth a little smile. Elizabeth realized with a jolt that Elizabeth's acceptance had assured Maria's. Unfortunately there was no way Elizabeth could try to kiss Conner with Maria around.

As soon as she had the thought, Elizabeth gave herself a mental slap. Was kissing Conner suddenly the only thing that mattered? *Get a grip, Wakefield.*

"Don't you have to work Friday night, Maria?" Tia asked. "You were just talking about it in homeroom this morning." Elizabeth's hopes rose a notch. Maria was too responsible to skip work for a concert. *So are you,* her conscience nagged.

"I'll figure something out. First and Ten can do without me for one night," Maria said, popping open a soda. "You're supposed to work too, right, Liz?"

Elizabeth ran her fingers through her hair. Maybe she should just go to House of Java on Friday. Tia's whole kissing plan was ridiculous, and Maria obviously wanted Conner back. The whole thing was too messy.

"Yeah. I'm not sure if I can get someone to cover for me," Elizabeth said reluctantly.

Conner bit into an apple. "You should come," he said with his mouth full. He didn't even look at her when he said it, but Elizabeth felt the magnitude of the statement. He never singled anyone out like that.

Elizabeth glanced at Tia's eager face, then Maria's pleading one. "Okay," she said. "I'm there."

And I'm going to get Conner alone if it kills me.

"I couldn't believe it, Liz," Jessica said into the phone that night. She stretched out on the

50

blue-flowered bedspread in her room at the Fowlers' and sighed. "No one bothered me at practice today. Of course, no one talked to me either, but it was an improvement." She leaned back against one of the plush throw pillows and closed her eyes.

"That's good," Elizabeth said. "Maybe we should have a party for Tia or something."

"I know. But I don't think anyone would come," Jessica said sarcastically. "She's getting the silent treatment too. I feel so bad."

"I doubt she minds that Cherie and Melissa aren't talking to her," Elizabeth said. "They're not exactly kindred spirits."

"Whatever that means," Jessica said with a laugh. She felt semi-lighthearted for the first time in days. No one had called her a slut. No one had picked on her clothes. She felt like a new, albeit invisible, woman.

"Hey, Jess, when was the last time we pulled a switch?" Elizabeth asked suddenly.

Jessica squinted. It almost sounded as if Elizabeth was *suggesting* a twin switch. "Why?" she asked suspiciously.

"I don't know," Elizabeth said slowly. "We just haven't done it in a while, and we used to have so much fun—"

"Who *is* this?" Jessica asked, sitting up straight.

"Jess—"

"What have you done with my sister?" Jessica asked, laughing. "I usually need to twist both your arms before you'll do a switch."

Elizabeth laughed too. "Yeah, I guess you're right. But I've changed my mind."

"Because . . . ?" Jessica prompted.

"I need you to work my shift at House of Java on Friday night," Elizabeth explained. "It's not that big of a deal, really. The job is pretty simple. And you can keep all my tips."

"Work?" Jessica rolled her eyes and picked at the fringe at the end of her blue throw. "Oh, goody."

"Please, Jessica."

"You know, when I used to make *you* do switches, you would always get to do something fun, like go on a date or something," Jessica said.

"Don't even make me remind you of how some of those dates ended," Elizabeth said.

"Good point."

Jessica flopped back on her bed and raised her knees. There was a time when she never would have given up a Friday night to work, no matter how much money was involved. But things had changed. Working at HOJ would give her an excuse not to spend another Friday night alone.

"OK, I'll do it," Jessica said.

"Yes!" Elizabeth exclaimed. "Thank you so much, Jess. If you ever need—"

"I was just getting to that," Jessica said.

"What's up?" Elizabeth asked.

"I'm supposed to work early Saturday afternoon, but I would have to tear out of there to get changed in time for the game," Jessica explained. "If you take my shift, I don't have to worry about being late and having Laufeld kill me."

"No problem," Elizabeth answered quickly.

"We're going to have to get together and prime each other on our jobs," Jessica said with a smile.

"Let's do it tonight," Elizabeth suggested.

"Okay. Why don't you come over for dinner?" Jessica said, starting to get excited. It had been ages since she actually had something fun to do.

"That last reception was beautiful, man," Trent Maynor said as he and Jeremy walked out of the Big Mesa locker room with the rest of the team.

"Yeah, well, your passing wasn't bad either," Jeremy responded with a weak smile. He pulled his varsity jacket on over his gray T-shirt. There was a huge banner hanging over the gym door that read Crush the Gladiators! The cheerleaders must have hung it while the team was practicing. Everyone was getting hyped on school spirit.

"Big Mesa rules!" Mike Petro cheered. He raised his fist as they headed out the double wooden doors. "SVH doesn't stand a chance against us."

"No doubt," Jeremy said. The guys roared their assent. Jeremy tried to get caught up in the excitement of the upcoming game—the first of the season. But as his friends pumped each other's egos around him, he felt hollow. It was like the first Christmas after he found out there was no Santa Claus. There was just this faint memory of past anticipation.

"Hey, guys!"

Jeremy and his friends turned to find two fellow seniors, Stephanie Mullen and Jennifer Crowly, walking behind them. Jeremy almost kept going. He had no patience for Stephanie and her stuck-up friends. But the guys stopped to allow the girls to catch up. Jeremy hung back from the crowd and waited.

"Hi, Jennifer," Mike drawled, draping his arm around her shoulders. He shook his thick, brown hair away from his face. "How was volleyball practice?"

"Fine," Jennifer said, smiling. "How was football practice?"

"We're a well-oiled machine," Mike answered. "So, when are you going to come over and help me with my calculus homework?"

She playfully shoved his arm away and giggled a response, adjusting the slim strap of her skimpy tank top. Jeremy shook his head and stared at the ground. The guys were only interested in these girls when they could get something from them.

He smelled Stephanie's strong perfume a moment before he felt her presence next to him.

"Hi, Jeremy?" she said.

"Hey." Jeremy looked up, and Stephanie struck a pose she must have practiced every night in the mirror. Head tilted just slightly so that her long, black hair fanned over her shoulder. Not too wide smile. Eyelids just slightly heavy.

Jeremy smiled and looked away so she wouldn't see the amusement in his eyes.

"A bunch of girls are wearing home jerseys to the game at SVH on Saturday?" she said.

"Yeah?" Jeremy tried to look interested. The fact that Stephanie lifted the end of every sentence as if it was a question always distracted him.

"Uh-huh. And I was just wondering? If no one had asked you yet? If maybe I could borrow yours?" She raised her perfectly plucked eyebrows.

Jeremy saw the guys mocking Stephanie behind her back. He felt his cheeks turn red. Nine out of ten of them had either kissed the girl or wanted to, but that didn't keep them from trying to look cool by picking on her.

Jeremy looked straight into her unnaturally violet eyes—colored contacts for sure. "Sure, you can borrow mine, Steph," he said. "I'll bring it in tomorrow."

"Cool," she said, grinning from ear to ear. "Thanks."

"No problem," Jeremy said, hoping a girl wearing his jersey didn't mean more than he thought it did. "Guys. Are we outta here?"

"Yeah, let's go," Trent said. He walked up to Jeremy and slung an arm over his shoulders. "I wanna buy my star receiver a burger."

"Bye, guys!" Stephanie and Jennifer called.

"Hey! I'll call you later!" Mike told Jennifer. She blushed and headed off toward Stephanie's red Mazda.

"Dude, are you really gonna call her later?" Stan Ramsey asked.

"Maybe. Maybe not," Mike answered.

The guys cracked up.

"What's up for Friday night?" Stan asked as they walked toward the parking lot. "My father's working late in LA, so my place is open."

"Nothing too crazy," Joe Datolli warned. "We have to pulverize SVH the next day."

Mike nodded solemnly. "Right. So we'll only get one keg." Everyone laughed as they reached Mike's black Ford Explorer. "I'll be in charge of getting the eats and brew," Mike said. "Lay your cash on the car."

Jeremy found himself hanging back again as everyone opened their billfolds and pulled out twenties.

Stan turned to Jeremy. "You in?"

Jeremy shook his head and stuffed his hands in

the pockets of his jeans. "I have to work Friday night."

"You never hang anymore," Joe said accusingly.

"Yeah," Mike agreed. "You think you're too good for us?"

"Basically," Jeremy replied jokingly.

"No, really. What's so great about working every weekend?" Stan asked him directly. "We have a *game* the next day."

Jeremy shrugged. "I told you guys—Dad's being stingy with the gas money. Gotta get around somehow."

"I guess," Mike said. They were all just staring at him. *They don't get it,* Jeremy thought. *They don't even understand being short on cash. Imagine if I told them I was paying bills.*

"I gotta go," Jeremy said, backing toward his car.

"What about that burger?" Trent asked.

"Rain check," Jeremy called over his shoulder as he jogged across the parking lot. He needed to be someplace that wasn't defined by lies. Jeremy paused as he pulled his keys out of his pocket. The problem was, he didn't know if a place like that existed.

Melissa sat at the counter at Rafferty's and sipped her diet soda, hoping she didn't look like a total loser. She glanced at the door for the hundredth time and then looked at the neon clock behind the bar. Will was more than twenty minutes late.

He's avoiding me, she thought. Her nerves were fried, but she smiled at a passing waiter in an effort to look calm. After yesterday's little argument, Will had been acting totally distant. He usually kept his arm around her shoulders or his hand on her back—constant contact. But today he'd barely even touched her. She'd felt naked standing near him.

The waiter leaned his elbows on the wooden surface of the counter. "Can I get you anything else?" he asked.

"No, thanks," Melissa answered. "My boyfriend should be here any minute." She looked at the door again. "Unless he's standing me up," she said under her breath.

"Who would stand you up?" the waiter asked with a friendly wink.

Melissa blushed. She hadn't intended for him to hear her, but he had a good point. She was being ridiculous. Will would never ditch her. He might have been in an accident or something, and here she was, harboring traitorous thoughts.

"You're right," Melissa said. "I think I'll go call him and make sure he's okay."

The bartender smiled at her, and she made her way through the restaurant to the pay phone by the bathrooms.

Will's mother picked up on the first ring.

"Hi, Mrs. Simmons," Melissa said.

"Oh, hi, Melissa," Mrs. Simmons answered. "Will's not here right now."

Melissa smiled. "Is he on his way to meet me?" she asked.

There was a pause, and Melissa unconsciously gripped the phone a bit tighter. "I don't think so," Mrs. Simmons said. "He said something about going over to Josh's house to play basketball."

"Oh." Melissa's humiliation temporarily squelched her powers of speech. "Maybe I got the time mixed up," she said, trying to save face. She didn't want Will's mom to think she was an idiot. "Did he say anything about meeting me at Rafferty's later?"

"Not that I recall. Maybe you should call him at the Radinskys'," Mrs. Simmons suggested. "I have the number right here."

"No. That's okay. I know it," Melissa said. "Thanks, Mrs. S."

"You're welcome."

Melissa hung up and held on to the receiver for a moment. Her heart was racing. She knew she didn't have the time wrong. She and Will were supposed to meet for dinner at eight. They'd only made the plan a few hours ago, before they both went to practice. Had he forgotten? He couldn't have left her sitting here purposely.

59

She picked up the phone and dialed Josh's number, jabbing at the keys.

Josh's little sister picked up the phone and ran to get Josh from the driveway before Melissa could tell her she really wanted to speak to Will. Melissa chewed on the inside of her cheek while she waited for Josh to pick up the phone. She heard the door slam and feet shuffling across the kitchen.

"'Lo?" He was out of breath.

"Josh, it's Melissa. Can I talk to Will?" she asked.

"Will?" Josh tried to catch his breath. "Will's not here."

Melissa's heart stopped. "Yes, he is," Melissa said. "His mom just told me he was over there, playing basketball with you guys."

"Well, he was—" Josh paused. "Hold on. Wait a minute."

Melissa could hear mumbled voices as Josh covered the phone with his hand. Then the sounds became clear again.

"Liss?"

"Will?"

"What's up?" He was panting too.

"Josh just told me you weren't there," Melissa said. Loud voices erupted from a nearby table, and she pressed her finger against her free ear.

"I just got here," Will said stiffly.

Melissa's head started to pound. "You just got there," she repeated. "It doesn't sound like it."

"What do you mean?" Will asked.

"You're as out of breath as Josh, so you were obviously playing—"

"I just got here and ran inside," Will interrupted.

"Whatever," Melissa said. "Did you forget you were supposed to meet me at Rafferty's half an hour ago?"

"God, Liss, I'm sorry," Will said, a bit too quickly. "I forgot."

Melissa took a deep breath. "Can you just come here now?" she asked.

She heard laughter in the background on the other end of the line and felt her skin heat up. *They're not laughing at you,* she thought. *They're just messing around.*

Will held the phone away from his mouth. "Will you guys shut up?" he demanded. Then he was back. "I promised the guys, Liss," he said. "They don't have teams without me."

Melissa felt tears spring to her eyes and ignored them. "You promised me," she said.

"I know," he said. "I'm sorry. I'll call you later, okay?"

He really wasn't coming. "Will, I—"

There was another burst of laughter. "Okay?" Will repeated in a whisper.

"Fine." She slammed down the phone. Melissa's heart was racing. She pushed through the bathroom door and walked over to one of the white porcelain sinks. She gripped the edges and stared at herself in the mirror, willing herself to calm down.

"He didn't just do that to me," she said. "There's no way he stood me up, lied, and then blew me off." She took a few deep breaths and told herself to just wait until later, when they could talk. There was no point in getting all freaked out right now when there was nothing she could do about it. As she rationalized, her anger started to subside.

Unfortunately it left behind a deep, sinking fear.

Conner McDermott

Look, I didn't want Elizabeth and Maria coming to this concert. All I wanted was to have a night out with my friends, support Gavin, and hear some kick-ass music. But lately Tia comes as a package deal with Elizabeth, and I knew I was going to get an earful if I didn't invite her. So fine. I can handle Elizabeth. It's not like I have to hang out with her all night, right?

But how was I supposed to know that Maria would say yes? I mean, is the girl a glutton for punishment? Why does she even want to be around me after the way I dumped her? Most girls turn all their friends against me and give me the evil eye for at least a month after a scene like we had.

But not Maria. Which means only one thing. She still wants me. Which means I'm gonna have to deal with her in my face all night. Her _and_ Elizabeth.

When am I going to learn?

Elizabeth Wakefield

Things to tell Jess re HOJ

People scheduled to work Friday night:

1. The owner, Mrs. Scott (probably will be hovering, as she always does on the weekends);
2. The manager, Ally Scott, Mrs. Scott's daughter (skinny with strawberry-blond hair);
3. Suzanne (middle-aged with short, brown hair and brown eyes) or Nancy (middle-aged with short, brown hair and blue eyes)—I'm not sure which one will be there;
4. Jeremy (very cute, with green eyes and short, brown hair).

Explain cappuccino machine! Note to self—draw diagram.

Go over all the different kinds of cakes, muffins, scones, biscotti, cookies, etc.

Make sure Jess knows where to find stirrers, different sugars, cups, mugs, milk, cinnamon, nutmeg, whipped cream, etc., etc.

Teach her to use the grinder, blender, teapot, foam thingy, etc.

Maybe I should tell Jeremy she's coming.

Jessica Wakefield

<u>Notes</u> <u>for</u> <u>Liz</u>

Recipes for all the shakes are in the blue binder by the blender.

If anyone asks a question about vitamins, read from the box without looking like you're reading from the box.

At the register, type in the price of an item and hit subtotal. After everything is entered, hit total. It adds tax automatically.

Working Saturday — Jim, the scrawny manager; Jordan, the Rasta; and Beach, the total babe.

CHAPTER
Overtime

"Ew! Jeremy, look!" Jeremy's twelve-year-old sister, Emma, sat back on the carpet and pointed at a damp, yellowish streak running down the length of his bedroom wall. Just what he needed to see when he was getting ready for work.

"Oh, man, not another one!" He groaned. The roof was already leaking in at least four other spots around the house. But it was Friday evening, and he was running late for work. There was nothing he could do about it now. It was a good thing it didn't rain often in southern California. He just hoped the roof didn't collapse on their heads before he and his mom had saved enough money to get it fixed.

"Too bad the earthquake bypassed this dump," Jeremy said.

"Seriously," Emma agreed, leaning forward again to rummage through the crate that held his CD collection. "Maybe you could have used the insurance money to buy some good music."

"Very funny," Jeremy said, plopping down on

his bed and pulling on his sneakers. "Why don't you go watch Trisha so she won't bug Mom while she makes dinner?"

Emma rolled her eyes, sucking at her braces. "Okay, fine. I'll go watch the brat." She paused at the door and threw her shiny, brown hair over her shoulder. "You're so lucky you get to go to work."

"Yeah, right," Jeremy said as his sister breezed into the hallway. He heard six year-old Trisha screeching in the kitchen and Emma trying to coax her out into the living room. His mom was banging around the pots and pans with extra vigor. Okay, so maybe he was a little lucky.

A soft knock sounded on his door. "Mind if I come in?" his father asked.

"Go ahead, Dad," Jeremy said, keeping his back to the door so his father wouldn't read the exasperation on his face. It was time for the drill.

"What are you doing?" As usual, his father seemed surprised to see Jeremy putting on his worn, brown, House of Java T-shirt.

Jeremy chuckled. "What's it look like?" he said good-naturedly.

"You work too much, Jeremy." His father folded his arms and leaned back against the door-jamb.

Somebody has to, Jeremy thought. "I don't work that much," he said.

"A guy your age shouldn't be wasting a Friday night," Mr. Aames continued. "You should be out having fun." He paused and ran a hand over his balding head. "You're only young once."

"Stop feeding me clichés," Jeremy said with a laugh. His father's worry-lined brow furrowed deeper, and Jeremy felt bad. He didn't want his dad to think he was teasing him.

"I have fun at my job, Dad," he said, stuffing his apron into his backpack. "I like working."

Mr. Aames shook his head. "It doesn't seem right to me. Don't kids today believe in parties and movies? And what about girls? Have girlfriends gone out of style?"

"No, Dad," Jeremy said with a smile. It was time to put on the peppy act and bring this week's father-son chat to a close. "Actually, that's the best part of my job. The place is always packed with girls."

His dad raised his eyebrows. "Oh, really?"

"Sure," Jeremy said. "Not to mention the fact that I get to work with a gorgeous blonde."

"Aha! The truth comes out," his dad said, flashing him a man-to-man grin. "I knew it wasn't all work and no play at that coffeehouse. So tell me about her. What's her name?"

"Elizabeth," Jeremy answered. "She's gorgeous—blue eyes, pretty smile. She's smart too, and nice." He glanced away from his father's probing look. Not that he was guilty of lying or anything. There actually was a girl named Elizabeth who worked with him at House of Java, and she did fit the description.

Jeremy had simply left out the fact that he wasn't interested in her as more than a friend. She was fun to work with, but that was all. He had enough on his mind these days. The last thing he needed, or could afford, was a girlfriend.

"Sounds perfect," Mr. Aames said.

Jeremy pulled his bag onto his shoulders. "I gotta go," he said.

His father stepped away from the door, but he grabbed Jeremy's arm as he tried to walk through. Jeremy froze, knowing there was some assertion coming. Some promise about how things would get better.

"I just don't want you to feel like you have to work, Jeremy," his father said.

Jeremy glanced into his father's sad brown eyes and looked away again. He hated that he was supposed to reassure his father that everything was fine. He was only seventeen. He wasn't ready for the parent-child role reversal yet.

"It's fine, Dad," he said.

"I hope you won't let this job get in the way of your schoolwork or football practice. This is your senior year. Your grades and your game are going to matter more than ever when it comes to getting into college next year."

Then get off your butt and get a job so I can con-centrate on my life, Jeremy thought. *Actually call for some of those jobs you're constantly circling in the classifieds.*

"Got it covered," Jeremy said. "Everything is great at school, and I'm playing better than ever."

"Good," Mr. Aames said with a sad smile. He released his grip on Jeremy's biceps. "I'm looking forward to your game on Saturday."

"Yeah, me too," Jeremy said. "I really gotta go."

"Have a good night!" his father called after him.

Once safely inside his car, Jeremy let out a deep sigh of relief.

"Another outstanding performance by Jeremy Aames," he muttered. *Maybe I should drop football and join the drama club.*

Sweep mascara to middle of lashes, hold to set curl . . . count to three. . . .

"I can't believe I'm reciting this stuff," Elizabeth muttered to herself. "No more fashion magazines for a while."

There was a loud pounding at the bathroom door. Elizabeth jumped and drew a jagged streak of mascara across her forehead.

"It's time to go!" Conner yelled.

"I'll be out in a second," she responded as evenly as she could manage. No need to start the evening off with a battle, considering she was hoping to kiss the jerk before it was over.

She quickly repaired the damage, gathered her things, and rushed into her room for one more look in the full-length mirror.

Not bad, she thought. She was wearing heeled, black ankle boots; a pair of black, slim-fitting knit pants; and a blue-green tank top that matched the shade of her eyes. It also revealed a few inches of her stomach, which unnerved her a little. Elizabeth wasn't used to showing off extra skin. She pulled her black cardigan out of her closet and shrugged into it. Suddenly she looked dowdy. She pulled it off again, dumped it on her bed, and walked out of the room without looking back. It was time to start taking risks, even if they were tiny ones.

Elizabeth walked into the kitchen, where Conner, Evan, Andy, Tia, and Angel Desmond were waiting.

"Nice outfit!" Tia exclaimed.

"You look drool-worthy, my friend," Andy commented.

"Five hours in the bathroom," Conner grumbled, grabbing his wallet and keys. "She should."

Elizabeth turned to Conner with an exaggerated sweet smile. "Five hours ago I was in French class, conjugating irregular verbs."

"Don't mind him," Tia said, wrinkling her nose

at Conner. "He's grumpy when he hasn't been fed."

"Thanks, Tee," Conner said, clearly annoyed. "Can we go?"

"Shotgun!" Evan called, leading the way into the foyer.

Elizabeth took a deep breath and mentally ran through her lines as everyone headed for Andy's mother's silver minivan.

Conner, why don't you drive too—since we both need to come back here anyway? It would be stupid for Andy to have to drop us off when we'll be getting home so late. Even if he didn't drive her *to* the concert, he'd have to drive her home. Guaranteed kiss opportunity.

Tia slid open the rear door, and Conner was about to climb in.

"Conner—"

"What? Did you forget your lipstick or something?" he asked.

Elizabeth reddened. "No. I just thought maybe you should drive too—"

"Why?" Andy asked. "It's no fun if we don't all ride together."

"Yeah. There's plenty of room," Evan said, climbing into the front seat.

"It's not the room," Elizabeth said. "It's just—"

"We've fit at least this many people *and* Andy's fat, disgusting dog lots of times," Angel remarked.

"Casey is not disgusting!" Andy countered

74

indignantly. "She's just a bit high-strung."

"And slobbery," Evan said, leaning out the window.

Elizabeth cleared her throat, clutching her small purse. "But Conner and I—"

Conner sighed and shrugged into his beat-up, brown suede jacket. "I don't feel like driving," he said. "We're gonna miss the first set if we don't go."

Elizabeth opened her mouth to try one last time, but Andy cut her off.

"We still have to get Maria," he said. He climbed into the driver's seat and slammed the door.

"You think *she'll* slobber on us?" Evan said, laughing as the engine roared to life.

Tia groaned. "You guys are so immature. I can't take you anywhere." She disappeared inside the van.

Elizabeth gave up and climbed in. It was pointless anyway. Conner's attitude was far less than attractive tonight. If he kept acting like this, maybe she'd get over him without the kiss.

Angel and Tia were already cuddled into the backseat. Conner was sitting next to the window on the front bench. His arms were crossed, and he was staring out at the driveway.

"Relax, Conner. We'll get there in plenty of time," Tia said, kicking the back of Conner's seat. Elizabeth sat down next to him and leaned over to pull the door closed.

"Yeah, man," Angel said. "Chill out."

"Okay," Conner said. "Let's just go."

Andy started the engine and pulled out of the driveway. Elizabeth glanced at Conner out of the corner of her eye and was fully relieved her little plan hadn't worked. She felt as if there were a wall of ice separating her and Conner. Alone in a car with him would not be a fun place to be.

What was I planning to do anyway? Kiss him at a red light? Elizabeth thought. *Moron.*

"Hey! Let's play the license-plate game!" Tia said excitedly.

Elizabeth laughed. Conner could be as moody as he wanted. She was just going to kick back and have some fun.

"She's such a loser," Cherie said, bringing her black coffee mug to her lips. "She thinks she's so cool just because she has an older boyfriend, but did you hear he didn't even go to college because his father spent his tuition money?"

"That's not true," Will said, shifting in his seat.

"What?" Cherie snapped.

Will took a deep breath and told himself not to rip Cherie's smug little face off. This was not his idea of a fun way to spend a Friday night before a game, but he'd promised Melissa he'd make up for ditching her. Now he was trapped at House of Java with Melissa and her obnoxious friends while the rest of the team partied.

"Angel and Will are friends, remember?" Melissa said, slipping her hand over Will's under the table. "They played basketball together."

"I didn't realize you still hung out with him," Cherie said.

"I don't, really, but that's not the point—"

"Angel just deferred school for a semester to make some spending money," Melissa interrupted calmly.

Will was glad to hear Melissa defending someone for once. "Yeah. Just because his family isn't well-off, that doesn't mean there's something wrong with him," he said. "The guy has a full scholarship to Stanford."

"Sorry," Cherie said, finishing off her coffee. She glanced at Gina Cho, who rolled her eyes. "Tia's still a loser."

Will leaned back in his chair and stared at the door. The guys were all over at Todd Wilkins's house, having a mini-psych-up session. They were probably playing video hockey, scarfing Taco Bell, and going over that afternoon's practice. Will would buy the whole café a round of coffee if it meant he could get over there.

"Will? Can you get me another latte?" Melissa asked.

Now he was errand boy? Will took a deep breath. He was just overreacting to everything because of the tension he'd felt around Melissa lately.

But it was just a phase. All relationships went through this. It would pass.

"Are you sure?" he asked. "Don't you want to sleep tonight?"

Melissa smiled. "You're right."

Will sighed. At least he had avoided taking orders.

"How about a decaf?" Gina suggested, smirking at Will.

"Yeah. How about a decaf?" Melissa repeated.

Will pushed his chair back abruptly and stood. "Can I get anyone else anything?" he asked sarcastically.

"No, thanks!" Cherie and Gina said in unison.

Will walked over to the counter and pulled out his wallet. *Just chill,* he told himself. *They can't drink coffee for much longer.* Maybe he should tell them all their teeth were turning yellow. They were too vain to ignore something like that.

"Hey, man."

Will looked up to find Jeremy Aames, the Big Mesa football team's captain, standing behind the counter in a green apron.

"What's up?" Will said. He only knew the guy by reputation, but he was sure Jeremy knew who he was too. "You ready for tomorrow?"

"You know it," Jeremy said, smiling as he wiped down the counter. "Can't say this is the best way to get primed for a game, though," he added.

"Seriously." Will glanced over his shoulder at the girls. "I should be hanging with the team right now."

Jeremy laughed. "Me too. There's a pretty decent party going on. If I had a choice, I would not be here," he said.

Will straightened up. "Yeah. You're right."

"Can I get you something?" Jeremy asked.

"Decaf latte," Will said. Jeremy filled the order, and Will pocketed the change.

"Good luck tomorrow," Jeremy said as Will walked away. "You'll need it."

"Yeah, right," Will answered. "Make sure you bring a lot of body bags." Jeremy laughed, and Will was smiling as he returned to the table. The kid might be the enemy of the moment, but he had a point. Will should be with the team. It was the night before the first game—a game against Sweet Valley's biggest rival. He was letting the guys down just by being here.

Will set the latte on the table and pulled his jacket off the back of the chair.

"Where're you going?" Melissa asked, her eyes wide.

"I'm gonna go over to Todd's," Will said. "The guys are going to be pissed if I don't show."

Melissa stood up and pulled Will away from the table. He straightened his collar nonchalantly.

"You're just gonna leave?" she hissed.

"Liss, you know this is really important," he said, not expecting his argument to make a difference. He had to put in the effort, though.

"And I'm not?" she asked, her blue eyes clouding. "After what you did the other night—"

"I apologized fifty times for that!" Will said. "What do you want me to do? I can't diss the team on the night before the first game."

Melissa crossed her arms in front of her and looked away. Will almost walked out. He wasn't sure what he was waiting for. He doubted she was going to give him her blessing to leave. But then, surprisingly, her shoulders sagged.

"You're right. I'm sorry," she said. "You're probably nervous, and being with your friends will help."

"Right," Will said, ready to accept any explanation. "Right."

"We can spend time together tomorrow," Melissa said with a small smile.

Will barely heard her. In his mind he was already on the road. "Thanks, Liss," he said. "I'll talk to you later."

He was out the door and halfway to his car before he realized he'd forgotten to kiss her good night.

Will Simmons

I don't usually stand people up, so ever since I left Melissa sitting alone at Rafferty's, I've been trying to figure out why I did it. Because I knew it was wrong even <u>while</u> I was doing it. So how could I be such a total jerk? Well, it just hit me, so here it is:

Lately when I'm with Melissa, I feel like I'm suffocating.

I always thought that was an expression—that people who said stuff like that were just exaggerating. I thought it was impossible to be in love with someone and feel like you were closed in—gasping for air. Because if you love someone, you want to be with them.

You don't feel like you _have_ to be with them. You don't feel like they're your responsibility.

The thing is, I've always sort of felt like Melissa was partially my responsibility. Part of our relationship was me taking care of her—looking out for her. It's only lately that I've felt . . . trapped. And it's not a feeling I like.

CHAPTER 6
A Near Miss

Jessica walked into the back room at House of Java that evening and bumped into a middle-aged woman with short, brown hair and red-rimmed glasses.

"Sorry," she apologized, racking her brain for a name.

"No problem, Liz," the woman said, grabbing a couple of sugar dispensers from a supply shelf.

There was also a younger woman with a strawberry-blond ponytail sitting at a small desk. Ally, the manager. At least she remembered that. "Hi, Ally."

"Hey," Ally said with a brief smile. "Listen, you guys, be on your toes tonight. Mom's on the warpath."

"What do you mean?" the woman asked.

Ally stood up and straightened some papers. "End of the month, we're running out of everything, she thinks we're using too much sugar, milk, blah, blah, blah. The usual. I'll see you out there." She pushed through the door into the café.

"It's gonna be a fun night," the woman said sarcastically.

"Yeah." Jessica studied her. *Suzanne has blue eyes, Nancy has brown . . . or is it the other way around?* "I didn't realize you were working tonight," Jessica hedged.

"Yeah. Suzanne called in sick, but I'm sure she's faking. I saw her at the beach this afternoon with a new guy."

Nancy! Jessica thought. "A new guy?" Jessica said as she hung up her jacket. "That's interesting."

The woman glanced at her. "I guess. You look like you're in a good mood tonight."

"I am," Jessica replied, although it was a serious understatement. She was beyond joyous—all because she was working her sister's shift on a Friday night and wouldn't have to spend the time cooped up at the Fowler mansion. "But I should be seeing a shrink," she said under her breath.

As Nancy left the room, Jessica put her backpack on one of the shelves in the coat closet, just like Elizabeth had instructed. Then she signed in on the clipboard attached to the wall. Her hands were shaking, so she clasped them together.

"Don't be nervous—just figure out what comes next," Jessica said. She looked around, trying to remember. Should she stock something? Or fill something? Or—the back room was bigger than she thought it would be. The walls were lined with

84

shelves of supplies. Next to Ally's little desk and bulletin board were a beat-up maroon couch and low table with magazines strewn all over it. At the back of the room were two doors. One was metal and obviously led to a walk-in refrigerator, and the other was made of wood and unmarked. Of course, nothing gave Jessica a clue as to what she should be doing.

The door was flung open and a gorgeous guy was standing there, all smiles. "Get your apron and get out here, Wakefield. I'm tired of covering for your late butt."

Jessica's heart was so busy skipping, she almost forgot how to formulate a sentence. "Apron, right. Okay, I—I'm not late, am I?"

"No. I'm just kidding," the guy said. "Don't forget to wash your hands." And then he was gone.

"Hands. Apron. Right," she said to herself. She washed her hands in the small sink in the corner and shook them dry. "What was his name?" Jessica muttered as she grabbed an apron and tied it on. "Something with a J . . . Jeffrey? Jonathan? Jeremiah?" It didn't matter. She had to get out there.

The J guy was behind the counter. He glanced at her and smiled.

"Mrs. S. is already here, so it's a good thing you actually are on time tonight," he said.

Jessica didn't respond. Was Elizabeth, the Princess of Punctuality, usually late?

"Good evening, Elizabeth," a clipped voice said.

Jessica turned around to find a heavyset woman with short, blond hair and far too much eye makeup standing behind her. Where had she come from?

"Hi . . . Mrs. Scott," Jessica said.

"I just wanted to let you know I'm keeping an eye on everything tonight," she said, lowering her lids into a glare. "I don't want to see you handing out free coffee to that sister of yours."

Jessica turned a deep shade of crimson. *I guess I should stop bumming drinks off Liz,* she thought. "Don't worry. Jessica won't be here tonight."

"Good." Mrs. Scott turned on her heel and disappeared into the back room.

"I should have warned you she was hiding in her office," *J* said.

Her office? Where was that? Jessica mentally reviewed her image of the back room and remembered the plain wooden door on the far wall. She had assumed it led to the alley behind the building, but it must be an office. Weird.

"So, how are you tonight?" *J* asked. "How's your man?"

"My *man?*" Jessica repeated. Elizabeth didn't have a man. What was her sister telling these people? Then she noticed laughter twinkling in his green eyes—*gorgeous* green eyes.

"I'm just kidding," he said, tossing her a thick

paper cup. Surprised, she fumbled with it and knocked it around before she finally caught it. "Someone's not on the ball tonight."

"What's this for?" she asked.

"For your coffee," he responded.

"Oh. I don't want any." She set the cup down near the sink behind the counter.

"You will," he said, grinning. "By the end of the night, you'll need it."

His smile was infectious. Jessica felt as if she'd landed in paradise.

Suddenly, finally, his name came to her.

"Thanks for the warning, Justin," she said, relieved her memory had finally kicked in. She turned to one of the machines to make herself a latte. It was time to relax and start perfecting the other aspects of the job.

Conner climbed out of the van and stretched his arms out to his sides. "Nice parking, Marsden," he said.

"Thanks," Andy said, patting the hood of the van. "I knew there had to be a space up here somewhere."

"Sorry I doubted you," Conner said.

Elizabeth smiled and looked at the crowds streaming toward the coliseum. "It looks like mood-swing boy has swung back toward happy," she muttered to Maria.

"Seriously," Maria agreed. "My fingers are frostbitten from being in the same car with him."

Elizabeth took a deep breath. *Try sitting between him and his ex,* she thought. When Maria had climbed into the van, she'd opted to squeeze in next to Elizabeth rather than join the lovebirds in the backseat. Consequently Elizabeth had been too close to Conner for comfort. He had spent the whole ride shifting around, staring out the window, and sighing through his nose while Maria had darted glances at him every five seconds.

"You're in a better mood," Tia said to Conner.

Conner glanced at Elizabeth and Maria. "I was sick of sitting in the car."

Elizabeth looked at Maria, but she seemed to have missed the significance of the statement. Obviously Conner had been uncomfortable about being near one or the both of them.

"I have to go pick up the tickets from the reservation window," Conner said as they all started to walk toward the stadium. "Does anyone know where it is?"

Elizabeth looked around at her friends' blank faces. She hesitated for a split second before answering. "I do," she said. Conner's eyes flicked at her. "My dad gets tickets for the basketball games from his company sometimes. That's where we pick them up."

"Great!" Tia said. "You can show Conner where it is while Angel buys me some food."

"I was waiting for that," Angel said, hugging Tia from behind. "This girl can cram more junk food than you can imagine."

"There's a vendor right over there," Evan said. "I could use some grub."

Elizabeth looked at Conner, sure he wouldn't want her company.

"So let's go," he said.

"Okay." Elizabeth glanced at Maria, who just shrugged. "We'll be right back," Elizabeth said.

"C'mon, Maria," Andy said, crooking an arm around her neck. "I'll buy you something really unhealthy."

Conner started walking, so Elizabeth fell into step with him.

"I'm so psyched for this," Conner said suddenly. Elizabeth was startled. She'd expected the same silent treatment he'd given everyone in the car.

"This is a big deal for Gavin, huh?" she asked.

Conner looked at her, and his eyes were actually dancing with excitement. "No one deserves a break more than Gavin does," he said. "He's been trying to get a shot like this for years."

"That's really great—"

"Watch it!"

Elizabeth tripped over a curb, and Conner reached out to steady her. He grabbed both her elbows. Elizabeth gripped back reflexively. "I'm such a klutz."

Conner released her. "You okay?" he asked.

"Yeah," she said, straightening her shirt.

"C'mon," Conner said. "I think I see the window."

Elizabeth was still blushing from her graceful maneuver when they joined the line. She never seemed to fail to do something stupid when Conner was around. But instead of smirking at her or making a comment like he usually did, Conner was still talking about Gavin and his lessons. She'd never heard him say so many words in one breath. She almost pinched herself to see if she was having some bizarre dream. Conner was sharing. With her.

"Conner, can I ask you a question?" Elizabeth asked as the line inched forward.

His eyes clouded momentarily. "What?"

"Does . . . does being around Maria make you uncomfortable?" Elizabeth asked.

Conner looked away. "Why would it?" he asked.

"I don't know. . . . It's just . . . in the car—"

"I was just tired of being stuck in there," Conner said. "It's no big deal."

"Okay." Elizabeth wrapped her arms around her waist, covering her bit of exposed skin. "It's just, maybe if you told her how you really feel—"

"God! What is it with you?" Conner's eyes flashed. "Why do you have to make everything into some big issue?"

"I'm sorry," Elizabeth said. "But why do you

have to jump down my throat every time I ask you a question? I just wanted to help."

They reached the window, and Conner gave his name. "I don't need your help," he said more calmly. The man behind the window slid the tickets across the counter. Conner picked them up and shoved them into his back pocket. "Let's just go back and find everybody."

Elizabeth nodded and followed Conner as he wove through the crowd. *So much for just relaxing and having fun.* When was she going to learn to keep her big mouth shut?

"Here you go, *Elizabeth,*" Jeremy said as he added another cappuccino to her tray. It was hard to say the name and keep a straight face.

"Thanks for making these for me, Justin," she said.

That did it. Jeremy turned away so she wouldn't see him laughing. Elizabeth had told Jeremy that her twin sister would be filling in so that he could help her out if she needed it. But it seemed that Elizabeth had neglected to tell Jessica that he knew, because she was keeping up her charade with him.

Jessica was good, he had to give her that. She had Elizabeth down pat—the pencil behind her ear, the quick, bouncy walk, the slight tilt of her head as she explained the difference between the double-roasted, mocha house blend, and the Dutch Royal mocha blend for the tenth time in one hour. The only thing she'd messed up on was his name.

"Maybe I should tell her I know," Jeremy said under his breath.

He watched Jessica carry the tray over to a table of obnoxious college guys, all of them jerks with I'm-too-cool attitudes. Jeremy wished he'd waited on them himself. They were the kind of customers that usually put Elizabeth in a bad mood.

But Jessica didn't seem irritated at all. She passed out the coffee, smiling the whole time, then stayed and talked with them for a few seconds. When she walked away, they were considerably less loud.

"Congratulations," Jeremy told her when she came back to the counter.

Jessica narrowed her eyes. "What do you mean?"

"The way you handled those jerks," Jeremy said.

Jessica turned away, busying herself with cleaning off her tray. "Yeah, well . . . jerks are my specialty."

It was an offhanded comment, but Jeremy could tell there was more behind it. She'd been hurt recently. He didn't know why he knew—he just did.

"What did you say to them?" Jeremy asked.

"I told them you'd beat them up if they didn't behave," Jessica said with a slow smile.

Jeremy felt himself starting to blush and grinned. "Yeah, well, I could see how that would scare them," he joked. He flexed his biceps, and Jessica rolled her eyes.

"Oh, yeah, you could take them," she said. She grabbed a rag and started wiping down the counter. "In your dreams," she added in a stage whisper.

Jeremy tapped her shoulder. "You wanna go? Right now?" He assumed a boxer's stance, and Jessica dropped the rag.

"You so don't wanna go there," she said, laughing.

Jeremy straightened up and dropped his arms. "You're a black belt or something, right?"

Jessica opened her mouth to respond, but suddenly her eyes darted at the door and all the color drained from her face. Jeremy turned around and saw two slim girls walking into the café—one with long, straight brown hair and the other with equally long, straight blond hair. He'd seen Elizabeth talk with them a couple of times.

"Do you know them?" Jeremy asked.

"I gotta . . . um . . . go to the bathroom," Jessica said. "I'll be right back."

She shoved through the door to the back room just as the two girls got to the counter.

"Wonder where Elizabeth was going in such a

hurry," blond girl said as they studied the menu on the wall behind Jeremy.

"She's probably all mad at us because of Jessica," brunette girl said with a laugh.

Jeremy looked back at the door Jessica had disappeared through. What were these girls talking about? What was Jessica so afraid of?

"Excuse me," brunette girl said. "We'd like to order now."

"Lila!" blond girl said, swatting her friend's arm.

Jeremy narrowed his eyes slightly. Lila. Nice attitude. Whoever this girl was, he definitely didn't like her.

Megan Sandborn

The way I figure it, Conner and Liz should be together by now.

I know Elizabeth likes him, so I figure it's his fault they don't get along. It's not surprising, though. Conner is an absolute moron when it comes to girls.

Take Maria, for example. That relationship had an even shorter shelf life than I predicted. Maria's cool. And she's smarter than the girls Conner usually goes out with. I thought he'd give her at least two weeks before he found a flaw and chucked her. But they didn't even get that far. I don't know why exactly they broke up, but I figure she probably told Conner she loved him or something and he wigged. That would be standard Conner. I think he's a walking fear of commitment.

Actually, that might be why he's so mean to Elizabeth. He probably knows she's the coolest girl he's ever met and is afraid he'd actually <u>want</u> to make a commitment to her, so he won't let himself get too close.

Hey! That's not a bad theory. Maybe I should study psychology.

Or maybe I've just been watching too much <u>Oprah.</u>

CHAPTER 7
Close Encounters

"I am so sick of *Seinfeld*," Justin said, reaching around Jessica to get the cinnamon shaker. His arm brushed against hers, and she almost shivered. Was that a move?

Get real, Jess, she told herself. *He was in need of cinnamon.*

"I know," Jessica agreed. "They show it three times a day. No one can take that much George."

She poured hot water into a teapot and set the carafe back on the burner. *Earl Grey and rhubarb cheesecake,* she repeated to herself. She had the rhythm down. It was all in the choreography, like cheerleading. She took out a slice of cake from the cooler, drizzled a circle of strawberry syrup around the edge of the plate, and added four dollops of whipped cream.

"I think I've seen that episode with the Jon Voight car at least a hundred times." Justin rang up his sale and went over to check the coffee carafes. "Looks like we need more Jamaican blend and French decaf."

"There are so many other good shows they could rerun," Jessica said. She added a tea bag and mug to the tray and placed it on the counter.

The elderly customer glared at it as if it were poison. "Elizabeth, you *know* I can't eat this," she complained.

Jessica's heart thumped. This was obviously a regular customer. "You can't?"

"Of course not!" the woman said. She pulled her eyeglasses to the tip of her nose and studied the plate.

It's just a pop quiz, Wakefield. Take your time.

She'd followed Elizabeth's instructions exactly—one scoop of strawberry topping drizzled around the cake and four little plops of whipped cream. The plate looked clean.

Jessica was stumped. "I'm sorry—," she began.

"That's okay, honey." The lady gave her a friendly smile and pushed the plate away a few inches. "We all make mistakes."

Justin placed another slice of rhubarb cheesecake minus the strawberry topping on the counter. "I think I grabbed your order by mistake," he said with a smile. He took Jessica's plate. "This is mine."

It was a beautiful save.

"Thanks," Jessica said when the woman walked away with her strawberryless plate. "I don't know why I forgot about the topping. She's allergic, right?"

"Yeah. But don't worry. It happens," Justin said.

"Right," Jessica said. "I could have killed her."

"Mrs. Rischeck is always on the ball. She'd never eat it without inspecting it first." He lifted her plate in front of her nose. "The good news is, we get to eat this now."

Jessica's eyes lit up, and she grabbed a fork. "I'm starving."

Justin set the plate on the counter, and they both went at the cake in full force.

"You seem a little out of it tonight," Justin said as he cut into the slice.

"What do you mean?"

"Well, you kind of bolted when those girls walked in here before," Justin said. "Are you okay?"

Surprised, Jessica glanced at him to see if he was joking around again. His eyes were full of concern. He cared. He actually cared.

"You can talk to me, you know," he said quietly, his eyes never leaving her face.

In that moment Jessica believed him. She felt she really could tell him everything. He seemed like the kind of person who would actually listen—who understood the importance of secrecy. But then a thought hit her like a lead balloon. He wasn't extending the offer of friendship to her. He was extending it to Elizabeth.

She turned away. "I'm fine," she said. "I guess I'm just a little tired."

The bells above the door tinkled, and Jessica looked up, relieved to have customers to distract her. But her relief was short-lived.

Aaron Dallas walked in with two El Carro guys she recognized from the soccer team—and from the times they had mocked her in the hallway at school. *Not again,* Jessica thought. *I'm busted.* She'd been dreading this moment all night. She couldn't legitimately disappear into the bathroom again, especially now that she knew Justin had noticed her odd behavior.

They're going to destroy me in front of Justin, she thought. In full panic mode, she purposely knocked a box of straws to the floor and bent to retrieve them, hoping the guys would pass her by.

"Hey, Liz." It was Aaron's voice.

Jessica stood up slowly. Aaron looked at her . . . and smiled.

"What?" Jessica said.

Aaron laughed, but it was a nice laugh, not a mocking one. "I said, hey. How's business?" They were the most beautiful words she'd ever heard. Jessica felt light enough to float to the ceiling. Of course. He was expecting to see Elizabeth, so that's who he saw. He had no reason to look closer.

"Good. Thanks for asking," Jessica said, trying to keep the emotion out of her voice. "What can I get you?"

As Aaron and his friends placed their orders,

Jessica took a deep breath and let it out slowly. Everywhere else she went, her problems dragged behind her like heavy metal chains. But here she was free to talk to people—to have fun and laugh without risking cold stares and insults.

House of Java suddenly felt like a gift.

"They're amazing," Tia said. "Gavin is so good."

"Yeah." Elizabeth craned her neck to see down the long line outside the bathroom. She leaned back against the cool, gray brick wall. "Really good." *Unlike this night. This night is really bad.*

"So, Maria." Tia bounced up and down on the balls of her feet, grinning. "What's up with you and Evan?"

Elizabeth watched a fake smile spread across Maria's face. "I don't know," she said coyly. "He's kind of cute."

"You've been flirting with him all night," Elizabeth pointed out as she inched forward with the line.

"I have not," Maria responded, giving Elizabeth a playful shove. She was acting giddy, but Elizabeth could tell it was just *acting.*

Yes, you have, Elizabeth thought. *You've been flirting with him to make Conner jealous, and it's making everyone ill.*

"Hi, Evan!" Maria called out.

Conner and Evan were walking by the line, and

Evan turned and strolled over to Maria. Conner slowly followed.

"You guys have already been to the bathroom?" Tia asked, still bouncing up and down. "Being a girl is so unfair."

"We were just going to get something to eat before Silver Chair comes on," Conner said.

"Do you guys want anything?" Evan asked.

"Evan, you know what you could get me?" Maria said excitedly. She laid one hand against his chest. "I would *love* a snow cone."

"Okay," Evan said, backing away slightly. Elizabeth felt her stomach turn. Maybe she should help Maria save face and tell her to stop. "Elizabeth, do you want anything?"

Elizabeth smiled. "No, thanks. I'm good."

"You sure? I don't mind," Evan said. Conner looked off down the concourse, and Maria stared at the floor.

"I'm really not hungry," Elizabeth said. "But thanks."

"Okay." He smiled at her.

"Let's go," Conner said, starting to walk off.

"You can get me a hot dog!" Tia called after them.

Conner lifted a hand in response.

"Jeez," Tia said. "I'm, like, inviso-girl around you two."

Elizabeth looked at Maria, and they both

laughed. "Sorry about that," Elizabeth said, glad the tension was broken.

"You know what? This waiting around is making me insane," Tia said. "Do you guys want to go crash the men's room?"

"I'm there," Maria said. "I'm going to burst soon."

"I don't think so, guys," Elizabeth said.

"Why? Are you chicken?" Tia teased.

"No," Elizabeth lied. "I just feel like I've already put in my time here. Why waste it?"

"Suit yourself," Tia said. She backed away from the line. "Come on, Maria."

"Sorry, Liz. I really have to go," Maria said.

"It's okay," Elizabeth replied. When they'd gone, Elizabeth felt relaxed for the first time all night. *Alone in the crowd,* she thought. Conner hadn't spoken to her or Maria since the scene at the ticket window. Elizabeth had thought through their conversation a million times since the concert had begun, and she'd come to one conclusion. She could never ask Conner a question again. Ever.

When Elizabeth was finally done in the bathroom, she headed back to the seats. On her way to their section, she spotted Conner by himself at one of the souvenir stands.

Her heart started to race. He couldn't ignore her if they were alone.

What is wrong with you? she thought. *Do you like being yelled at?*

Elizabeth turned abruptly and bumped into a large man carrying a tray of food. Luckily nothing spilled.

"Sorry," she said. He muttered something and walked off. She had to start paying attention to little things like walking. She cut a straight line through the thinning crowd until she was standing next to Conner.

"Hey," she said.

"Hi." He barely even looked at her.

"Here you go, man." The guy behind the counter dropped a black T-shirt on the counter.

"Where's Evan?"

Conner turned to her, his eyes hard. Great. She'd thought that was an innocent inquiry. It had nothing to do with Conner.

"Inside," Conner answered, pocketing his change. "He bought you a lemonade."

Elizabeth's brow creased. "But I told him I didn't want anything."

"Yeah. Go figure," Conner said with a smirk. He grabbed the T-shirt and started making his way back toward the entrance to their section.

Elizabeth rushed to catch up with him. Go figure? What was that supposed to mean? *I would ask him, but he'd probably bite my head off,* Elizabeth thought. She walked alongside Conner in silence for a moment, but she couldn't take being ignored again.

"Is that for Megan?" she asked.

"Yeah." He stopped abruptly and turned to Elizabeth with a serious look in his eyes. "Elizabeth, can I ask you a question?"

Please don't let him be mocking me, Elizabeth thought. She'd said the exact same thing to him earlier. "Sure," she replied.

"Do you know how to get a mustard stain out of clothes?"

Elizabeth blinked. "What?"

Conner looked down at her chest, and Elizabeth felt her face turn beet red.

She glanced down and saw a yellow glob clinging to her dry-clean-only top like a giant mutant amoeba.

Elizabeth tried to cover with a laugh. "I just bumped into this guy—"

When she looked up again, Conner was gone.

Her embarrassment turned to anger. She walked over to a concession stand and grabbed a napkin to clean herself with.

"Hey, Liz!" Tia appeared at her elbow. "C'mon. They're going to start soon." Tia looked into her face and frowned. "What's wrong?"

"Nothing," Elizabeth said with a sigh, wiping the blob off her shirt. "I just should have gone to work tonight."

"What do you mean?" Tia asked.

Elizabeth balled up the napkin and tossed it toward a garbage can. "Just remind me never to try to have fun," she said. "It's obviously not my style."

"One mocha cream coming right up," Jessica said, grabbing a nutmeg shaker from under the counter.

"Not a mocha cream. A double mocha, dark," the customer said.

"Oh, right," Jessica answered. "Double mocha—"

"Miss! Miss! I just want some extra sugar!"

"There's sugar on the station behind you," Jessica said.

"It's empty," the woman answered.

Mrs. Scott came out of the back room just in time to hear the customer's comment. Jessica's shoulders tensed. The woman had been hovering all night but not lifting a finger to help. "Empty?" she asked Jessica. "How much did you put out?"

Count to ten, Jessica told herself.

"I'll get the sugar—you get the mocha," Justin said, flying by her with a full dispenser.

"Thank you," she said, rushing to one of the coffee machines. "Where's Nancy?"

"On break," Justin shouted back over the din of the customers.

"Great," Jessica said. "Where's Ally?"

"She'll be out in a minute. She's arguing with the delivery guy."

"Miss!"

Jessica looked over her shoulder at yet another angry face. "One second," she said. Scalding liquid splattered onto her hand and she jumped, shattering the coffee mug against the counter. "Damn!" Jessica shook her hands.

"Lovely," Mrs. Scott said. She picked up the pieces of the mug, tossed them in the garbage, and walked into the back room.

Justin was by Jessica's side in a flash. "Run it under warm water," he said, pulling open a cabinet and removing a bottle of Bactine. Jessica shoved her hand under the faucet and took a deep breath to hold back the tears. *House of Java, a gift?* she scoffed at herself.

"This is a nightmare," she said, turning away from the sink. Justin reached out with a towel and dried her hand. Holding it for an extra moment.

"Are you okay?" he asked.

"No," she answered.

Justin removed the towel. "This is gonna sting." He sprayed her hand with the Bactine, and Jessica jumped back.

"Ow! You could have warned me how much it was going to sting," she complained, shaking her hand again. Tears burned her eyes.

"Sorry," Justin said.

"I'm back!" Nancy rushed behind the counter, tying on her apron.

"Thank God," Jessica muttered.

Justin reached out and touched her arm gently. "Why don't you go back to the storeroom and get some milk? Take a breather while you're there."

Jessica smoothed back her hair and pushed through the stockroom door. Elizabeth had neglected to mention the psychotic Friday-night crowd. The last hour had passed in a blur of spilled drinks and indignant customers. "I'll have to remember to thank her later," Jessica mumbled.

She rushed through the storeroom to the walk-in refrigerator in the back. The milk came in ten-gallon plastic bags, which were set into sturdy carrying cases. She lifted one gingerly, then hoisted it up into her arms. It was heavy and awkward.

"Liz! We need that milk!" Nancy's voice called.

"Coming!" Jessica quickly negotiated her way back through the stockroom with her arms stretched around the milk case.

She heard the door swing open. "Do you need any—"

"Watch out!"

Justin slammed into her, and before Jessica could even realize she was falling, she was on the floor. The bag of milk hit the tiles right next to her and burst, covering her in freezing-cold liquid.

"Oh my God! Are you okay?" Justin reached out his hand, obviously trying not to laugh, and stepped in the milk. Suddenly his foot slipped out from under him and he hit the red-tile floor with a loud thump.

Jessica froze. "Are *you* okay?"

At that moment Justin burst out laughing. That did it for Jessica. She let loose and laughed so hard, her eyes filled with tears and her whole body shook. Cold drops fell on her face, and she realized it was milk dripping from Justin's hair. She tried to tell him, but she was laughing too hard to say the words.

Justin dragged himself up to a kneeling position and tried to help Jessica. But they slipped on the wet floor and toppled over again, laughing hysterically.

"What is going on in here?"

Jessica looked up to find Mrs. Scott standing over them. She and Justin both fell silent. Mrs. Scott's eyes were practically popping out of her head.

"Do you know how much that milk costs?" she screeched.

Jessica looked at Justin and they both keeled over, laughing and gasping.

"You two are done for the evening." Mrs. Scott shook her head. "Clean up this mess and sign out."

"No, wait! We can stay!" Justin said between guffaws.

"Yeah! It's crazy out there. You need us!" Jessica agreed, trying to regain control.

"Not looking like that, I don't," Mrs. Scott said.

She pushed through the door, and Justin shot Jessica a concerned glance. Her heart fell. Sure, the tension was broken, she was tangled on the floor with a cute guy, and she was going to get home early. But what if she'd just gotten Elizabeth fired?

Andy Marsden

Here's why I think I could be qualified to write for a soap opera. Ready?

Maria spends the whole night flirting with Evan to get Conner's attention. Evan, who obviously isn't Maria's type, spends the whole night subtly trying to get Elizabeth's attention by playing the gentleman—offering her food, giving her his seat, helping her out of the car. Elizabeth, however, is oblivious to the fact that Evan is being very un-Evan-like on her behalf because she's too busy hoping Conner will say one word to her and hoping that he's not actually jealous of Maria and Evan.

Meanwhile Conner _is_ jealous of Evan, just not of Maria and Evan, because Conner is smart enough to notice that Evan has a thing for Elizabeth and not Maria. And Conner obviously has some kind of feelings for Elizabeth even though Maria is the one he dated. Of course, Conner and Elizabeth are living together and who knows what goes on over there.

Thank God, Tia and Angel are stable people.

no one's Sleeping Tonight

"Milk shampoos are supposed to be good for your hair, right?" Justin said as he held open the door for Jessica.

"You bet," Jessica responded, giggling. "I'm really sorry."

"It's not your fault," Justin said. "I wasn't looking where I was going."

"You're right. It was your fault," she said. She tried to smooth back her semiwet hair, but a warm evening breeze kept whipping it into her face. She dropped her hands and shoved them in her pockets.

Justin looked at her with a serious expression.

"I was just kidding," she said quickly.

"I know. It's just—" He reached over and pulled his hand through her hair. Jessica's scalp tingled at his touch. When he pulled away, he shook his hand at the ground. "You had coffee grinds in your hair."

Jessica reddened with embarrassment. "Oh." She took a deep breath of the balmy night air and sighed. Her stomach still ached from laughing . . . and it felt great. She slowly started walking down the sidewalk. She'd parked her mom's car around the corner.

Justin brushed a few grinds from his jeans and followed. "Well, at least you're not crying," he said.

"What do you mean?" Jessica asked, her brow creasing as she searched her bag for her keys.

"You know, it's no use . . . crying over spilled milk."

Jessica closed her eyes and shook her head. "You did not just say that!" she cried.

"Sorry. It had to be done." Justin shrugged helplessly.

Jessica laughed as she reached the blue Ford Taurus. "This is me," she said. "You don't think Mrs. Scott is really mad, do you?"

"She'll get over it," Justin said. "She's not gonna fire us or anything."

Jessica opened the car door, threw her bag inside, and slammed it shut. She wasn't quite ready to leave yet. "You think?"

"Nah. She needs us," Justin said. "She hates interviewing. She thinks it wastes time and that wastes money."

"That's good," Jessica said. *Maybe Elizabeth won't have to kill me after all.*

"Well, I'm parked over on Boulevard," Justin said.

At that moment Jessica really didn't want him to go. This was the most comfortable she'd felt in weeks. She'd hardly even had a conversation with anyone her own age other than Elizabeth. And Justin was a lot cuter than her sister.

"Justin, I have something to tell you," Jessica said. She paused and took a deep breath, wondering how he was going to react. "I'm not Elizabeth."

He raised his eyebrows. "Are the two of you related or something? Because you look a lot like her."

"Very funny," Jessica said. "We're twins. I'm Jessica."

"I know," he said. He paused and kicked at the ground. "I knew all along, actually."

"You did?" Jessica asked. "What gave it away?"

"Well, it was partially your good taste in television and partially the fact that you're twenty times better looking than your sister—"

Jessica's heart raced. She couldn't believe he'd just said that.

"But mostly it was the fact that you've been calling me Justin all night."

Her heart stopped racing. "What?"

"Jessica, I have something to tell you," he said with mock seriousness. "I'm not Justin. My name's Jeremy."

"I got your name wrong?" Jessica asked.

"Don't worry. I forgive you," he said, cracking a grin.

114

"Thanks," Jessica said, bringing her hand to her forehead. "I can't believe I did that. Jeremy."

"It's nice to hear you say my real name," Jeremy said. Jessica blushed and became very interested in her shoes. "So, why did you take Elizabeth's place tonight?" he asked. "You must have had someplace more exciting to be."

Yeah, right, Jessica thought. "Not really," she said with a shrug. "Elizabeth needed the night off, and it seemed like a good idea . . . until about five seconds ago."

"I think it was a great idea," Jeremy said softly.

Jessica's mouth went dry. He was giving her a definite guy-liking-what-he-sees look. Was he going to kiss her? Did she really want to kiss a guy who'd just seen her covered in milk?

"Well, I guess I should go," Jeremy said.

Or maybe he wasn't. She had to avoid getting her hopes up. She should just be happy to have a friend—someone who knew nothing about her reputation and didn't see a loser when he looked at her.

"It's been fun," Jessica said.

"Yeah," he agreed, taking a step back. "I'll see ya."

Jessica popped open the car door and climbed inside, trying not to watch him walk away. "More fun than I've had in a long, long time," she whispered.

*　　　*　　　*

Elizabeth closed her eyes and tried to relax her headache away. Silver Chair had turned out to be a lot louder than she expected, but there was no way she'd get up for an aspirin and risk bumping into Conner in the bathroom. She'd had enough of him for one day.

"At least he said good night," Elizabeth muttered to herself, pulling her fluffy white comforter up under her chin. "That must have taken a lot of effort."

The phone rang, startling her. She flipped over and grabbed it immediately, hoping it wouldn't wake Megan and Mrs. Sandborn.

"Hello?" Elizabeth whispered.

"Liz? It's Maria." Elizabeth squinted at her bedside clock. Maria sounded ridiculously perky for 3 A.M. "You weren't asleep, were you?"

"No. What's up?" Elizabeth asked.

"What did you think of Conner tonight?" Maria asked.

"I thought he was even more rude than usual," Elizabeth said truthfully. "Why?"

"Yeah, but did you notice him watching me?" Maria said. "Maybe I'm imagining things, but he seemed jealous of Evan. What do you think?"

"Maria . . ." Elizabeth had no idea what to say. Was her best friend going brain dead? If Conner had noticed Maria flirting with Evan, Elizabeth hadn't seen him exhibit any jealousy. He'd made a

116

point of focusing on nothing but the stage all night.

"So do you think there's still a chance for us to get back together?" Maria asked. "Because I really got the feeling that he was—"

"Maria, I thought you said you were over him," Elizabeth reminded her.

"I know." Maria paused. "I guess I lied."

Elizabeth sighed. "Just be careful with Conner, okay?" she asked, rubbing her forehead. "After the way he treated you—"

"You're right. I know you're right," Maria said quietly. "I just can't help it."

I know the feeling, Elizabeth thought.

"Anyway, I'm sorry for calling so late," Maria said. "I'll talk to you tomorrow."

"Okay. Good night, Maria."

"Night."

Elizabeth hung up the phone and took a deep breath. Somehow it seemed that her head was pounding even harder than before.

Jessica was smiling as she lay awake, staring at the ceiling. Who would've thought that serving overpriced coffee and cake for a few hours on a Friday night could change a girl's entire attitude about life? For the first time in weeks the huge guest room in the Fowlers' mansion didn't feel like a prison cell.

"Jeremy," she whispered to the empty room.

Jessica knew that meeting Jeremy didn't change the fact that she'd have to face her problems again very soon. Tomorrow was the Big Mesa game, where she would have to cheer in front of the whole school with Melissa by her side, ready to trip her or kick her in the face or something. But now she at least had a friend.

"Of course, I'll probably never get to hang out with him again," Jessica said with a pang of remorse.

She turned over and snuggled under the covers, refusing to feel sad. There'd be plenty of time to be miserable later.

Suddenly the phone rang. It was probably for Lila, but Jessica grabbed it anyway. It would give her some pleasure to hang up on one of Lila's jerk friends.

"Yeah?" Jessica said curtly.

"Hi, Jess?"

"Liz?" Jessica sat up and pushed her bangs out of her eyes. "What's wrong?"

"Nothing," she answered. "I was just wondering if you could do me another favor."

Jessica frowned. "You don't sound too good."

"I just got back from LA and I'm really tired." Elizabeth paused. "And my head hurts. Is there any way you could work my morning shift at House of Java too? I'm supposed to be there at seven, and

118

the way I feel right now, I don't think there's any way I'll be able to drag myself out of bed that early."

"Yeah, I guess so," Jessica said. She was too tired to get up and start jumping for joy, but the idea of working with Jeremy again made her giddy. "Aren't you at all curious about how it went tonight? You're usually not this calm about our switches."

"I'm too exhausted to care right now," Elizabeth said.

"That *really* doesn't sound normal."

"I'm fine," Elizabeth insisted. "At least I will be after I've slept for a few hundred hours."

"Just don't be late for my shift at Healthy," Jessica said.

"I'll be there," Elizabeth promised.

Jessica hung up and burrowed back under the covers. "I hope he's working tomorrow," she whispered.

She drifted off to sleep with her fingers crossed and a smile on her face.

Melissa shakily pressed the play button on the answering machine again and turned the volume down slightly so her parents wouldn't wake up. She chewed on her bottom lip as the tape clicked into gear.

"Liss? It's me."

Melissa held her breath at the tone of Will's voice. "It's not gonna change no matter how many times you listen to it," she told herself.

"I just got back from the party. I—I thought you'd be there."

"Yeah, well, maybe you'd know where I was all night if you hadn't ditched me," Melissa said. She'd only gone over to Cherie's to hang out, but still.

"Listen, we have to talk. I mean, I really need to talk to you."

This was where her heart kept hitting her shoes. She wasn't stupid. She knew what "we have to talk" meant.

"I'll meet you in the parking lot after the game, okay? Bye."

Melissa hit the stop button and stood in the middle of the kitchen, trembling. "What's going on with you, Will?" she asked the empty room. "Is it me? Or is it Jessica?"

Elizabeth Wakefield

The good news (if you want to call it that) is that Conner is speaking to me again.

And what did he say? "Lookin' good, Wakefield."

The bad news is the reason why. I rolled out of bed at approximately twelve noon and knocked on my bathroom door. Conner said, "Come in," so I figured that meant he was on his way out the other side.

Not so lucky. I looked at him, standing there all showered and clean and awake, and he looked at me, smirked (of course), and said, "Lookin' good, Wakefield." After he closed the door behind him, I looked in the mirror, and here is an inventory of what I saw.

One huge whitehead on my chin,
   Two frighteningly large smudges of
mascara beneath my eyes,
   About a hundred red lines running
<u>through</u> my eyes,
   A knot the size of Wisconsin in the
back of my hair,
   and
   A pillow crease as deep as a levee
running across my forehead.

   You know what? I don't think that
kiss will be happening. I think Tia needs
to come up with a new plan.

"Good morning!" Jessica said as she breezed into House of Java at six forty-five the following morning. The sun was already shining brightly, and a couple of gorgeous surfer babes walked by on their way to catch the good waves before the beach got crowded. Jessica had never experienced an early Saturday in her life, and it was oddly refreshing.

"Why are you like that?" asked a girl sitting at one of the front tables. She had black hair pulled into three ponytails and dark makeup surrounding her eyes. She was slumped over a steaming cup of coffee.

"Like what?" Jessica asked, heading around the counter.

"Never mind. If you don't know, there's nothing I can do for you."

Jessica shook her head and walked into the back room. She went right for the schedule and scanned the list of names. "So that's either Corey or Daniel." She pulled an apron over her head. "I'm guessing Corey." The next thing she noticed was that Jeremy wasn't on until nine.

"Bummer," she muttered, signing in.

Jessica fluffed her hair and walked back into the café. Something was different. Everything looked . . . bare. Where were the straws, and the napkins, and the sugar packets? That was when Jessica realized Elizabeth's instructions hadn't covered the morning routine.

"What do I do?" Jessica muttered to herself.

"Try taking out the mugs. You're probably gonna need them."

Jessica smiled and looked up. Jeremy was standing in front of the counter, holding a white paper bag and grinning from ear to ear. "I brought breakfast," he said.

"I thought you weren't coming in until nine," Jessica said.

"Oh, so now you're checking my schedule," Jeremy said. "Does this mean I have a potential stalker?"

"Don't flatter yourself," Jessica said, leaning on the counter.

"Mrs. Scott called and asked if I'd come in early," Jeremy explained. "I figured after last night, I'd better try to make nice."

"Good idea," Jessica said.

"Anyway, we open in half an hour, so we'd better eat this now." He climbed onto a stool and opened the bag.

"This place is packed with pastries. Why did you buy breakfast?" Jessica asked.

Jeremy pulled out two egg sandwiches and two bottles of orange juice. "I was in a good mood this morning, and I felt like splurging," he said. "This is for you." He pushed one of the sandwiches toward her.

"Oh, this looks good," Jessica said. "How did you know I was going to be here?"

"A guy can hope," he said with a smile.

Jessica's heart flipped. There were certain signals she couldn't ignore or pass off.

"Ugh!" A grunt came from the direction of the front table. Jessica looked over at Corey, who was holding her head in her heavily ringed hands. "Are you guys, like, dating now or something?"

"Me and Liz?" Jeremy said. He looked back at Jessica and winked. "Nah. Elizabeth and I have nothing in common."

"I never even met Jeremy until late last night," Jessica added, trying to keep a straight face.

"What?" Corey asked, looking disgusted.

Jessica and Jeremy laughed.

"You people are really weird," Corey said, standing up and crumpling her paper cup.

The door flew open, and a tall guy with a blond crew cut walked in. "What's up, guys?" he asked.

"Here's the update, Danny," Corey said, pulling her plaid skirt down slightly over her fishnet stockings. "Those two are wacked, and I'm going to the czar's office to take a nap."

Corey clomped around the counter, passing

Jessica and leaving the smell of lingering cigarette smoke behind her. She walked into the back room, slamming the door behind her. "What's her deal?" Jessica asked, wrinkling her nose as she sipped her orange juice.

"She's Mrs. Scott's daughter," Daniel said.

"You're kidding," Jessica said. She looked at Jeremy. "*She's* related to Ally?"

"No joke," Jeremy said. "Corey's a natural blond."

"I think she's Satan's love child," Daniel put in, pulling off his denim jacket.

"Then I guess it all makes sense," Jessica said.

Daniel joined Jeremy at the counter, threw his jacket over a stool, and grabbed half of Jeremy's egg sandwich. "So," he said to Jessica. "Who are you?"

Jessica blushed and stopped chewing as a lump formed in her throat. She was caught.

"See?" Jeremy said, raising his eyebrows. "I told you it was obvious you weren't Elizabeth."

"How could you tell?" Jessica asked Daniel.

"Easy," Daniel said. He popped the last bite of his sandwich into his mouth. "You're better lookin'." He winked, then walked behind the counter and disappeared into the back room.

"Told ya," Jeremy said.

"We're twins!" Jessica responded with a laugh.

"I didn't say I could explain it," Jeremy said. "That's just the way it is."

Jessica's heart flopped, and Jeremy's face turned beet red.

"I think I'll go sign in," Jeremy said, grinning as he crumpled up the paper bag from breakfast and gathered up his used napkins.

Jessica shivered as he passed behind her. This was going to be an interesting morning.

Elizabeth stepped out of the shower and started to towel dry her hair. The phone rang, and she paused to hear if anyone was going to pick it up. It rang again. And again. She threw on her fluffy pink robe and sprinted across her room, diving for the phone before the voice-mail system picked up.

"Hello?"

"Hey, Liz. It's Andy."

"Hey," Elizabeth said. She stretched the cord across the room and grabbed her towel out of the bathroom. "What's up?" she asked, patting her face dry.

"I just wanted to find out if Conner gave you my message," Andy said.

Elizabeth paused. "What message?"

"Figures," Andy said with a quick laugh. "I'm having people over today to hang out by the pool. It's beautiful out, so no excuses. I called this morning and told Conner to tell you."

Elizabeth's heart twisted. Conner probably didn't want her there and had purposely neglected to tell her. Either that or he'd been so frightened by her appearance at noon, the invite just slipped his mind. "He didn't," she said.

"Don't take it personally," Andy said. "I don't think the guy has ever taken the time to write down a phone message in his life."

Elizabeth smirked. "That doesn't surprise me."

"Anyway, he's coming," Andy said. "And I called a bunch of the guys . . . oh, and Maria's coming."

"Really? Maria?" Elizabeth winced when she heard her tone. She sounded jealous. Actually, she felt a little jealous. Andy calling Maria on his own meant that he thought of her as his friend. Maria was starting to become part of Elizabeth's new crowd.

And you're starting to become immature, Elizabeth told herself.

"So you should come," Andy said.

"What about the game?" Elizabeth asked.

"I'm not exactly a football person," Andy said. "And Conner wouldn't be caught dead displaying school spirit. Besides, Tia said she didn't care if we showed, and she said she'd hook up with us later tonight."

Elizabeth's brow creased. "I feel like I was supposed to do something today," she said. She was so overtired, her thoughts were all fogged.

Andy laughed. "Well, if you don't come up with it, come over," he said.

"Okay. Thanks for calling back, Andy," she said.

"No problem."

Elizabeth hung up the phone and sat on her

unmade bed for a moment. If Andy had called this morning, Conner had probably known about the party when he'd seen her in the bathroom earlier. He could have just told her then. Why was he so hot and cold with her? One second he was inviting her to a concert that was obviously important to him, the next he was avoiding telling her about a crowded, run-of-the-mill party.

"Whatever," Elizabeth muttered. Maybe she would just do him a favor and not go to the party. She was tired of always wondering how he was going to treat her—of getting her hopes up and then having him snap like he had the night before.

Elizabeth pushed herself up and started to walk back to the bathroom. On the way, something caught her eye. There was a piece of paper taped to her open bedroom door.

Elizabeth walked over and pulled down a note.

Liz—

Andys having everyone over to swim. 1 o'clock.

22 Akers Ave.

—C.

Elizabeth grinned. "Never writes anything down, huh?" she said.

Apparently she was now an exception to one of Conner's many rules. Unreal.

She tossed the note on top of her dresser and rushed back to the bathroom. If she was going to a party, she was going to have to figure out how to cover up that zit, fast.

"Biscotti and scones are basically the same," Jeremy told Jessica. They were standing outside House of Java, and he was groping for things to say, stalling because he didn't want to say good-bye.

Jessica pretended to give the matter some serious thought. "I'm sorry—I can't agree with you. They just don't taste the same."

"Think about it." He tried not to stare at her, but this was the first time he'd seen her in sunlight. Her blue-green eyes sparkled, and her smile was unbelievable.

She was incredibly beautiful. He'd always thought Elizabeth was pretty, but he'd never seen her the way he was seeing Jessica. There was something deeper behind Jessica's bright eyes. And she seemed more guarded somehow. Less everything's-gonna-be-all-right than Elizabeth, who always seemed to know exactly where she was headed and how to get there.

Jessica also had a dry sense of humor he loved.

"I have thought about it, Jeremy," she said, folding her arms. "Scones and biscotti are not equal. Nothing alike. That's my honest opinion."

"Look at the facts," he said, putting on a professorial voice. "Basically they're two versions of overpriced dry bread, with a few nuts or chips thrown in to confuse people, both totally inedible unless you wash them down with—" A soft breeze fluttered through her hair, distracting him. *I should just go ahead and ask her out. That's why I'm still standing here, babbling like an idiot.*

"And there you have another major distinction," she said. "Scones are generally washed down with tea, biscotti with coffee."

Jeremy chuckled. "I didn't know that. But you're probably making it up, just like your theories of cross-pollination coffee flavors."

"Hey! That guy was asking too many questions," Jessica said. "I thought that was pretty good improvising."

"I'm sorry." He shook his head. "But the coffee business is tough, Jessica."

She gave him a tight smile. "I know. I just hope I make it one day. It's a dream." They fell silent for an instant, then burst out laughing.

Jeremy watched her laugh, loving the way her eyes crinkled. It had been ages since he'd felt so connected to another person. Even though he'd known Jessica for less than twenty-four hours,

Jeremy was sure that he could trust her, that she wouldn't judge him by the car he drove, or the friends he hung out with, or the position he played on the football team. She wouldn't look down on him because his father was unemployed and his house was falling apart.

But if Jeremy did ask her out, then what? Where would he take her? Two movie tickets, popcorn, and a tank of gas would set him back enough so that he wouldn't be able to pay the water bill this month. He'd paid four bucks for breakfast that morning and felt guilty. There just wasn't any way around it. He had too many responsibilities right now, and there wasn't much he could do to change that.

Jessica tucked a lock of her hair behind her ear and smiled up at him. "I should get going."

"Yeah, me too." He didn't want to go, but he had a game to warm up for.

"See you around, then," Jessica said.

He looked at her for a few more seconds, just studying her face. "See you later, Jessica," he said. As she walked away, he almost had to bite his tongue to keep from calling her back.

Conner McDermott

I finished reading <u>The</u> <u>Great</u> <u>Gatsby</u> for English class, and I'm supposed to write a report on it this weekend. Well, what can I say? It's just one more story about how a woman can mess up a mans life. It seems like a major literary theme. Not surprising.

CHAPTER 10
Part of My World

Jessica's high spirits fell as soon as she walked into the Fowlers' mansion. Lila was in the living room with her parents, showing off her cheerleading uniform, and her little twirling maneuver made Jessica want to hurl.

She tried to sneak by without anyone seeing her, but had no such luck.

"You're late," Lila said.

Jessica stopped and slowly turned toward the living room. "I know. I was at work," she said. *As if you care,* she added silently.

"I wish I could wait for you, Jess," Lila said, her voice sickeningly sweet. She walked into the hall and picked up her leather bag and pom-poms from the settee. "But I promised some of the other girls I'd pick them up." It didn't take a rocket scientist to guess who Lila was referring to.

"Don't worry about me," Jessica said with the same fake politeness. "I've gotten to plenty of football games without you."

Mr. Fowler appeared at the doorway, holding

his newspaper. "Lila, I'm sure you can wait for Jessica to get changed," he said.

Jessica felt her stomach turn. Mr. Fowler meant well, but he had no idea what he was suggesting. There was no way she was getting in a car with Lila and her friends.

"That's okay, Mr. Fowler," Jessica said, starting up the stairs. "I'm gonna be a while, so—"

Lila was already out the door, so Jessica didn't bother to finish the sentence. She walked into her room and threw her backpack on the bed. Actually, finding a ride today might be tricky. Her dad had driven her to work that morning and needed his car this afternoon. Elizabeth had the Jeep, and everyone else at school was treating her as if she were a walking contagious disease. Everyone except Tia.

Jessica dug the cheerleading phone list out of her bag and called Tia, but she'd already left. *Great. Now what?*

She was already running late. Taking the earlier shift at House of Java should have gotten her home in plenty of time to get to the game. But after she'd left Jeremy, she'd decided to walk home, not wanting to let the unfamiliar happiness she felt wane. Now she was just as rushed as she would have been if she'd worked her shift at Healthy.

Jessica had seen her mom's car in the driveway, which meant she was probably in her room or out by the pool. Maybe she would let Jessica borrow the Taurus again. She got up and changed into her uniform, then checked her reflection in the mirror. Seeing herself in her cheerleading uniform usually made her feel proud, attractive, and ready to have a great time. But not today. Jessica looked at her reflection in the mirrored closet doors and felt nothing but dread.

"This sucks," she said. Today's football game was the first of the season, the first of her senior year. Big Mesa was SVH's archrival. Everyone at school had been excited all week. Jessica should've been too.

But all she could think about was getting out there in front of the crowd. What if they laughed at her? Or booed her? Or what if she had to do a stunt and messed it up out of nervousness? She could just imagine the taunts that would start flying if she were carried out on a stretcher.

Jessica stared at her reflection. She looked the same, but inside she was a stranger to herself. Her old confidence had been replaced by uncertainty.

She took a deep breath, closed her eyes, and thought about the way she'd felt at House of Java that morning and the night before—comfortable in her own skin for the first time in weeks. And she'd made a friend. A gorgeous, sweet, funny friend who thought she was pretty and worth talking to . . . and might just ask her out at some point. Jessica opened her eyes and looked at herself again. Still the same. But there was a spark in her eyes that hadn't been there before. That was something.

Jessica grabbed her bag and headed downstairs. It was time to face the music.

Elizabeth pulled the Jeep to a stop behind Maria's red Cabriolet and killed the engine. There were so many cars on the street around Andy's house, she'd had to park about half a block away. Elizabeth had no idea Andy had that many friends. Not that it was surprising.

She pulled the keys from the ignition and noticed her hands were shaking. "What are you so nervous about?" she asked herself, tossing the keys into her wicker bag. She flipped down the visor and checked her reflection in the mirror.

The zit looked fine. It had taken her ten minutes, but she'd covered it up pretty well. Her hair was pulled back in a French braid, and her waterproof mascara definitely brought out her eyes. She looked great, so why was her heart fluttering?

It's the bikini, a little voice told her. Elizabeth touched her bare stomach beneath her T-shirt. She never wore bikinis—especially not in public. It just wasn't her thing. But when she'd seen this blue, flowered two-piece on sale, she couldn't pass it up. It was part of the brave-new-Elizabeth thing.

She just wasn't sure she was brave enough.

"Hey, Liz."

Elizabeth looked over to find Evan approaching from across the street.

"Hi," she said, flipping the visor back up.

"Are you going in?" he asked, pushing his sunglasses up to hold back his shaggy black hair. Elizabeth had never noticed his deep blue eyes before. He looked good in the sunlight.

"Yeah," Elizabeth said. She climbed out of the car and pulled her bag onto her shoulder. "Where are you coming from?"

"I live right there," he said, indicating a modest house with a perfectly manicured lawn. "I'm constantly over at Andy's bugging him for pool time."

"Oh. You like to swim?"

"Yeah. I'm actually on the swim team at school," he said.

Elizabeth was grateful for the distraction as they walked toward the house. Her heart skipped a beat when she saw Conner's Mustang parked at the end of the driveway. He was already here. She had been hoping she could get comfortable being out there in her bathing suit before he showed up.

"Can I ask you something before we go in?" Evan asked. Elizabeth could hear the sound of hip-hop music coming from the backyard, along with splashes and laughter.

"Sure. What's up?" Elizabeth asked.

Evan pulled his glasses off his head and fiddled with them. He looked at the ground, then at Elizabeth, then at something behind her head. Elizabeth barely noticed. She was too nervous about going inside. "You know what—forget it," he said finally.

"No. What is it?" Elizabeth asked. Maybe he wanted to ask her about Maria. Maybe he *was* interested after all and wanted to know what Maria thought before he went into the backyard and asked her out.

"Nothing," Evan said, putting on his glasses again. "Let's go out back. That barbecue smell is making me hungry."

"Okay," Elizabeth said, falling into step with him as they walked along a stone path by the garage.

"You look really nice, by the way," Evan said.

Elizabeth smiled, her self-image brightening. "Thanks," she said.

Evan grinned and opened a wooden gate for her. Elizabeth nodded her thanks and stepped through, glancing quickly around the pool area. She saw Maria standing with Andy by the grill on the other side of the patio. Luckily she didn't see Conner yet. She wanted to have a few minutes of comfort before she spent the rest of the day fully aware of where he was at all times.

"I'm gonna go say hi to Maria," Elizabeth said. "Wanna come?"

Evan's eyes flicked in Maria's direction. She looked up and waved. "Uh . . . sure," he said.

They walked around the pool, dodging splashes as they went. Elizabeth saw Maria's eyes go wide as they approached.

"Elizabeth Wakefield, are you wearing a bikini?" Maria said, a tad too loudly.

"Yeah," she answered, looking down at her white T-shirt and denim shorts. "How could you tell?"

"I can see the outline through your shirt," Maria said. She took a swig of her soda and smiled. "You go, Liz. I didn't know you had it in ya."

Elizabeth blushed and crossed her arms in front of her. "Well, now that you've made me so self-conscious about it . . . ," she said.

"Whatever," Evan said, grabbing a soda. "I'm sure you look great in any bathing suit."

Elizabeth blushed even deeper.

"Yeah," Andy agreed, flipping a burger. "Even one of those knickers jobs with the little hats and the puffed sleeves."

Elizabeth laughed and looked over her shoulder, wondering where in the crowd Conner was. She didn't know whether to hope he'd overheard the little conversation or not. It was embarrassing, but it was nice to know that at least Evan and Andy didn't think she was a dog.

*　　　*　　　*

140

Nothing like arriving in style, Jessica thought sadly as her mother drove her to the game. Her mom was going to a baby shower that afternoon, so she'd been forced to hitch a ride.

A senior cheerleader being dropped off at school by her mommy. Pathetic.

"Jessica, is everything okay?" Mrs. Wakefield asked, glancing at Jessica out of the corner of her eye.

Trying to smile, Jessica turned to her mother. "Sure, Mom. Why?"

"You just seem a bit down lately," Mrs. Wakefield answered. "And you're usually bouncing off the walls on game day."

Jessica's heart squeezed. She would love to tell her mother everything, but she'd already decided not to burden her parents with her problems. They had enough going on already. Plus she didn't exactly have time to spill the whole story right now.

"I guess I'm just nervous," Jessica said. "Coach is going to name the captain today." *Not that I have a chance,* she added silently. She looked up and realized they were a few blocks from the school. "You can let me off here."

"Why?" her mother asked, pulling the car over to the curb. "It's just up the street."

"We're all meeting at Annie's house and going to the game from there." It was a big, fat lie, of course. Jessica just didn't want anyone to see her in the Mommy-mobile. It would just be more ammunition to be used against her.

"Are you sure you're okay?" Mrs. Wakefield asked, putting the car in park. "If there's anything you want to talk about—"

"Mom, I'm fine!" Jessica said. Her mother fell silent. "I'm sorry. I didn't mean to interrupt you." Jessica leaned forward and gave her mom a quick hug. "I have to go."

"Okay, honey." Mrs. Wakefield smiled as Jessica pulled away. "Have a good time."

Jessica grinned back. "I'm sure I will." Another fat lie.

She waited for her mother to drive off, then began walking toward the school. Several cars honked as they sped past her. Jessica tried not to look up at the drivers.

A green van slowed as it drove by, and a couple of guys in Big Mesa jackets leaned out the window. "Valley scum," they shouted before screeching off.

"Real mature," Jessica muttered, but all she wanted to do was hide.

They must have thought she was so pitiful—an SVH cheerleader walking to the opening game all by herself. She didn't know how much more she could take.

The school parking lot was jammed full, and

people were flocking toward the back field by the hundreds. It was a perfect day for a football game—sunny and bright, with a soft, cooling breeze. Jessica could hear the band practicing in the distance. She smiled wistfully, feeling as if she were an alumnus coming back to see a game. As if she were already years detached from the spirit and excitement.

As she walked across the parking lot, Jessica managed to avoid making eye contact with anyone. She remembered the way she used to feel right before a game—the anticipation, the rush of adrenaline—but it didn't seem possible anymore. Too much had happened. Today the best she could hope for was to survive the ordeal.

Maybe I'll just cut through the gym and avoid the crowd, Jessica thought. As she walked by the girls' locker room, which the visiting football teams used during the games, the doors opened and the Big Mesa guys came running out, cheering and banging on the lockers. She jumped aside to avoid being knocked over and crushed by the herd.

"Jessica?"

She cringed at the sound of her name. One of the guys from school must have walked in behind her and was ready to start the day's mock-Wakefield festivities. Jessica whirled around, her fists clenched at her sides. *Take your best shot,* she thought.

One of the Big Mesa players broke away from

the pack and jogged toward her. *What?* Jessica thought. *The rumors have spread to Big Mesa now?*

When he reached her, he pulled off his helmet, removed his mouthpiece, and smiled.

Jessica blinked. "Jeremy?"

His eyes shimmered with laughter. "He's taking the day off. I'm Justin, the evil twin."

"I can't believe you're here!" she exclaimed, her heart pounding. "You play football?"

Jeremy looked down at his uniform. "Apparently," he said. They both laughed. "And you cheer."

"Every now and then," she said, grinning uncontrollably. It was so nice to see a friendly face in these halls. Her mood jumped from morose to giddy in about five seconds.

Then some movement behind Jeremy caught her eye. Melissa, Lila, and most of the squad were filing into the school. Lila spotted Jessica instantly and nudged Cherie.

Jessica froze as Cherie whispered to Melissa. Suddenly the situation didn't seem so wonderful. She'd wanted so much to keep Jeremy away from her miserable life, but he was standing right in the middle of it. He was a high-school guy—a *football* player—and very much a part of her world. And if Jessica knew anything about Melissa and her friends at all, she was sure Jeremy was about to discover exactly what her world thought of her.

"I have to go," Jessica said.

Jeremy's face fell. He reached out and grabbed her wrist. "Wait a minute—"

"I can't," she said, pulling away. "I have to go." She wrested herself free and hit the gym door with so much force that it flew open and slammed into the wall. She knew Jeremy probably thought she was a psycho, but she just kept moving. Jessica didn't want to be around to witness the loss of her only friend.

Coach Laufeld was standing beneath the bleachers with Tia, Annie Whitman, Amy Sutton, and Jade Wu. They were surrounded by pom-poms, megaphones, signs, and streamers. Laufeld wore her standard poker face. Melissa took a deep breath and looked at Cherie.

"Don't worry," Cherie said, tying her unruly red curls back. "In five minutes it'll be over."

"I know," Melissa said. Her palms were sticking to the plastic strands of her pom-poms. The stands were packed, and the band was warming up on the sidelines. Melissa knew no one was paying attention to the cheerleaders yet, but she felt like a bull's-eye on a dartboard. Why did Will have to pick last night to leave a message like that on her machine? It threw her off completely.

"Hi, girls," Laufeld said as Melissa and her friends approached. "Is Jessica here?"

145

"We just saw her downstairs," Lila said.

"Yeah. She was talking to some guy," Gina put in, dropping her pom-poms under the bleachers. "Surprise, surprise," she added under her breath.

Cherie, Lila, Renee Talbot, and Amy giggled, but Melissa stood on the track that ran around the field and rolled her eyes. There were more important things to deal with right now.

"She's probably just in the bathroom," Tia said, shooting Gina a scathing look.

Laufeld sighed and looked at her watch. "You girls are going to need to get out on the field with the banner soon."

"She'll be here," Jade said.

"I'm sure she will," Coach Laufeld agreed. She unzipped her SVH windbreaker and tossed it on top of her bag. "But I have an announcement to make, and I want to do it before you go out there."

Melissa's heart went into overdrive. *Finally,* she thought. *Just spit it out.*

"I had a very hard time with my decision," Laufeld said, clasping her hands in front of her—a standard lecture position.

Oh, well, Melissa thought.

"I've been watching you all very closely, and you're all doing a great job on your cheers, stunts, and dances, but the captainship isn't about skill. I need someone who exhibited leadership and school spirit and promoted unity. In the past couple of

146

weeks one person stood out in those areas, and you should all look to her as a role model."

Coach Laufeld's eyes rested on Melissa, and Melissa tried not to smile. There was nothing worse than a sore winner. Laufeld turned to her left.

"Your new captain is Tia Ramirez."

Melissa's insides hit the asphalt. Cherie reached out and squeezed her hand, but Melissa couldn't even squeeze back. She felt all her blood rush to her toes as Jade and Annie congratulated Tia. Melissa looked at Tia's beaming face, and her stomach turned.

It didn't make any sense.

Tia would never have even been considered for captain at El Carro. She'd always been a cheerleader, but she wasn't part of the pack. She didn't have the right image or the right attitude. She'd make a horrible captain.

"Tia, why don't you take your squad out there and set up for the team announcements?" Laufeld asked.

"Okay," Tia said with a laugh, releasing Renee from a hug. "Oh. But what about Jessica?"

"I'll send her out," Coach said.

As Tia and Annie picked up the long paper banner for the football team to run through, Melissa dropped to the ground and rummaged through a supply bag for red streamers, hoping to hide her face. Cherie knelt next to her. Melissa blinked back the tears that were threatening to explode from her eyes. She *was* the captain. She'd been named captain at El Carro High back in May before the earthquake. This shouldn't be happening.

"Are you okay?" Cherie asked.

"I can't believe this," Melissa said, standing up and walking toward the field, clutching a roll of streamers. "This has to be a joke."

"I know," Cherie said. "Tia? What was she thinking?"

Cherie and Gina flanked her while Lila and Amy brought up the rear. "It's so obvious what they did," Gina said.

"What do you mean?" Melissa asked, stopping in the middle of the field.

"Tia and Jessica," Gina said, her eyes flashing. "I'd bet money they told Laufeld about what happened at the pep rally. There's no other explanation."

Melissa's heart skipped a beat. Why hadn't she seen that before? "I feel sick," she said. Cherie put her hand on Melissa's back. "I knew it. I knew Tia would tell."

"And I'm sure Jessica convinced her to," Gina said. "Those two have been buddies lately. They probably went to see Coach together."

Melissa's memory flashed back to the afternoon when Tia had told her off. Jessica had been standing by the wall. Standing there gloating. She'd probably put Tia up to that public humiliation too.

"You guys? We'd better get over there," Lila said. "The team is coming."

Melissa looked up and saw the football team lining up behind the goalposts. Tia was grinning as she held one end of the sign for them. Melissa wanted to smack her smug little face so badly. Then her eyes roamed down the line of players. She picked Will out with no problem. He was bouncing up and down on the balls of his feet and shaking out his arms.

Melissa's heart squeezed painfully. She was trembling as she crossed the rest of the field with her friends to line up. She could hardly trust her knees to keep her going. Melissa's eyes flicked from Will to Tia and back again. He'd told her Tia wouldn't break her word.

But then again, he'd told her he'd always be there for her.

Will Simmons

The thing about being a quarterback is you can't hesitate. The second you take the snap, you have to put your play into action. If you hesitate, if you second-guess, you'll be sacked for sure.

But you also have to be prepared for the worst-case scenario. You know, if you're running a pass play and your receivers are covered downfield, you've gotta be able to think fast, read the defense. You've gotta know when to hand the ball off, when to throw it away, and when to just tuck the ball in and take your beating.

Coach says one of my best qualities is that I'm always

prepared for that worst case. I can always see the linebacker coming, and I always know what to do. And he's right—because I don't like to take my beating.

I wish I was like that off the field too.

CHAPTER 11
Girl Troubles

Jeremy felt like a traitor. His team had just gotten schooled by the SVH Gladiators. He had even fumbled once himself. And now he was trolling the enemy's sidelines, looking for one of their cheerleaders.

Jeremy shook his head and smiled. It was hard to believe that Jessica *was* a cheerleader. She didn't seem like the type. She had a sense of humor, but she wasn't exactly peppy the way all cheerleaders seem to be. She was more sarcastic than silly.

"God, listen to yourself," Jeremy said. He was always rallying against stereotypes, and now he was feeding into one. The fact that Jessica cheered just made her more interesting . . . and more difficult to figure out. Jessica would definitely keep him guessing.

He tried to be inconspicuous as he walked along the track, putting on a miserable, contemplative expression as if he were pondering the loss. A couple of girls in red-and-white pleated skirts ran by, and Jeremy's heart skipped a beat when he saw a bouncing blond ponytail. Then he realized the hair was much too long, and he sighed. Maybe Jessica was already on her way to the victory party.

Jeremy slowed his pace when he reached the SVH bench. The coaches were packing up, and there were still a few players milling around. He didn't really feel like getting his nose rubbed in the loss. Instead he stopped and scanned the bleachers. The crowd was thinning out, and he didn't see her anywhere.

Why did she run off like that before the game? Jeremy wondered.

He kept walking, kicking at crushed plastic water cups on the ground. He knew he couldn't have been the reason she suddenly bolted. She'd looked so happy when she'd seen him, and he hadn't had enough time to say *anything,* so he knew he hadn't offended her.

"Nice game, son." Jeremy looked up to find SVH's coach walking toward him.

"Thanks, Coach," Jeremy said. He shook the man's hand and smiled. "Not too proud of that fumble, though," he said.

"It happens to the best of us," the coach said, shouldering a huge duffel bag. "I'm sure we'll meet up with you again in the play-offs."

Jeremy nodded. "Lookin' forward to it." The coach excused himself, and Jeremy saw Will Simmons among the guys helping to gather the equipment. "Hey."

Will looked up and half smiled. "Hey, Aames. Who's the man now?"

"I guess you are," Jeremy said. "For now."

Will laughed, finished packing a headset into a black case, and snapped it shut. "What are you still doing up here?" he asked, picking up the bag and falling into step with Jeremy. "Shouldn't you be home sulking by now?"

Jeremy shrugged. "I was just looking for someone," he said. "But I think she's avoiding me for some reason."

"Oh, girl troubles." Will looked straight ahead as he spoke. "I have a few of those myself."

"Sucks, huh?" Jeremy said, swinging his helmet by the face mask.

Will paused. "Yeah." He had this far-off expression in his eyes, and Jeremy realized this was a serious relationship Will was talking about. Jeremy had never had a serious girlfriend, so he couldn't offer much advice. He felt pretty useless just standing outside the gym door with the guy while he brooded.

"Well, good luck, man," Jeremy said. "I hope it works out." He started to back away.

"Yeah. Thanks," Will said. "I'll see ya."

Jeremy turned and started walking around the school as Will entered the gym. He suddenly felt the need to just get out of there. Everyone was acting so weird today. First Jessica ran off with no explanation after they'd had a great morning at HOJ. Now perfect strangers were getting all emotional on him.

"Maybe it's a good thing I didn't find Jessica," Jeremy muttered to himself. After all, he'd already decided he wasn't boyfriend material at the moment—with no cash and no time. And if Will was any indication of how a relationship could affect a guy, he didn't want to have anything to do with it. He already had too much emotional baggage to deal with.

Still, he had a hard time imagining that Jessica could ever cause a guy to look that miserable. As he came around the corner, he saw a bunch of cheerleaders piling into a station wagon and paused to see if he recognized anyone. He wasn't ready to give up on her. Not yet.

"It's so disgusting to see those girls throwing themselves at him as if he were some kind of rock star," Maria said, flopping onto a yellow, flowered chaise longue.

Elizabeth didn't have to ask who she was talking about. Nor did she want to go there. "Do you want some pretzels?" she asked, passing Maria a bowl.

Maria shook her head. "Thanks, but I'm too nervous to eat. I wasn't even going to come, but . . ."

"How about a soda?" Elizabeth offered.

"But I shouldn't be nervous, huh?" Maria continued. "I mean, last night I made it totally clear that I'm over him and ready to move on. And I think he's even starting to realize exactly what he lost when he dumped me."

"Wait a minute—I thought you weren't over him," Elizabeth said.

"I'm not, but he doesn't know that," Maria said, stretching out her long legs. "I'm pretty sure I fooled him."

"Yeah?" Elizabeth asked distractedly. She moved an inch to relieve a crick in her back and had to adjust the bottom of her bathing suit for the hundredth time that day. She had yet to find a way to do it discreetly.

"He's probably just trying to make me jealous," Maria said. She pulled her black Audrey Hepburn sunglasses over her eyes and leaned back.

Elizabeth looked across the pool at Conner. He was sitting with two girls Elizabeth had seen around school, and they were talking and laughing about something. She couldn't hear them over the music and the splash fight in the pool, but just the scenario irked her—Conner hanging out with some random chicks when he hadn't even said one word to her all afternoon.

"Hey, guys!" Wendy Chen, one of the editors from the *Oracle,* fell into the seat next to Maria. "I wanted to talk to you about my article for the arts section."

"What's up?" Maria asked. Elizabeth saw the perfect opportunity to get away.

"I'm gonna go get some ice," Elizabeth said, pushing herself up. "I'm dying out here."

"You might want to stay, Liz," Wendy said, pushing her short, black hair behind her ears. "Give your opinion."

Elizabeth waved her off. "The arts section is Maria's deal." She hurried away before they could call her back.

Elizabeth felt conspicuous as she walked along the rim of the pool toward the cooler. She glanced at Conner out of the corner of her eye and saw him checking her out. Maybe the bikini was a good idea after all.

The cooler was stationed only a few feet from Conner and his admirers. Luckily Andy was standing nearby, so Elizabeth had a reason to hang around and eavesdrop. Unfortunately she didn't get the chance.

"Elizabeth!" Andy said, grinning broadly. "So glad you're here." He threw an arm around her, and his tone set warning bells off in Elizabeth's head.

"Why?" she asked suspiciously.

"We need another team member for pool volleyball," Andy said. "And you're it."

"Sounds like fun," Elizabeth said. Then she froze. Jumping around in the pool in this skimpy bathing suit? "But I don't really feel like getting wet," she said, maneuvering out of Andy's grasp.

"C'mon, Liz," Evan said, pulling off his T-shirt as he walked over. "Be on my team. We'll kick butt."

Elizabeth saw Conner glance at Evan's bare chest, then look at her.

"I'm really no good," Elizabeth said, backing away. "But thanks anyway."

"Elizabeth," Evan said. "You didn't come to a pool party to sit by the pool, did you?"

"Actually, I came for incredible company?" Elizabeth improvised.

Andy looked at Evan and smirked. Evan raised his shoulders in response. "She's going in," they said in unison.

Elizabeth's heart dropped to the ground. Evan and Andy inched forward as she inched away. "Oh, no, you guys. Come on." Elizabeth giggled nervously. She wanted to run, but she was surrounded by a maze of lounge chairs, beach bags, and sunbathing bodies.

"Here, Lizzie, Lizzie, Lizzie," Andy taunted her.

"We can either do this the easy way or the hard way," Evan added.

Elizabeth was aware that their antics were drawing attention. She looked around for help, and her eyes fell on Conner. He just stared back at her blankly.

"Guys, really——," Elizabeth said, putting up her hands.

Andy and Evan took the opportunity to grab her wrists. They pulled her forward, and Elizabeth let out one last yelp of protest, knowing she must look like an idiot. "I'm going to kill you!" she shouted at Andy, but it was too late. Elizabeth suddenly pitched forward and fell into the cool water with a very ungraceful splash.

While flailing for the surface, Elizabeth frantically made a checklist of her body. Everything felt covered, but it was hard to be sure. She yanked down on her top and pulled at the seat of her suit before coming up for air. Now she just had to murder Andy.

Elizabeth surfaced and pushed some stray hairs from her braid out of her face. She looked up and found Maria and Conner standing with Andy and Evan. Elizabeth was about to splash them all when a couple of guys nearby started laughing . . . at her.

Elizabeth looked around. Oh God. Was her bikini top around her neck or something?

Then Maria spoke. "Liz! Your face!"

Elizabeth's heart flipped. "What?" She glanced at Conner, and he covered his mouth and turned around. Elizabeth almost drowned herself. What was he laughing at?

"C'mere." Maria waved her over. "We'll go inside and clean it up."

Elizabeth was shaking as she dog-paddled to the metal ladder. "Clean what up?" she asked as she pulled herself out of the water.

"Wear much makeup?" one of the laughing boys asked.

"Liz, I'm so sorry," Andy said.

Elizabeth looked to Maria in a panic. Her hands flew to her face. What were they talking about?

"Mascara," Maria whispered. "It's all over you."

"She looks like she got her butt kicked," some guys said.

"Or she's hung over," another added.

"No wonder she didn't want to get wet."

Elizabeth took a deep breath and looked at Andy. "Bathroom," she said through clenched teeth.

Evan gingerly handed her a towel, and she snatched it out of his hands.

"Use the one upstairs," Andy offered. "All my mom's junk is in there."

Elizabeth wrapped the towel around herself, tucked her chin, and somehow made it to the house without running.

Will checked his watch and sighed, blowing his long, blond bangs out of his face. Where was Melissa? He'd already showered and changed, and she hadn't shown. Usually the cheerleaders had a brief meeting after a game. He was never done cleaning up before she was done going over next week's cheering strategy. As if there could possibly be one.

Things just haven't felt the same lately, Will mentally rehearsed for the hundredth time. It didn't matter, though. Nothing he said was going to go over well. She was going to lose it. Just imagine if he told her the real reason—that ever since they'd started school at SVH, he hadn't been able to stop thinking about Jessica Wakefield. He was lucky Melissa didn't carry Mace.

Will leaned back against his Blazer and looked at the front door of the school, willing her to walk through. His nerves were totally frayed. Part of him just wanted to go home and forget the whole thing. He fiddled with the key chain in his pocket, but he couldn't do it. It was time.

He was going to have to break Melissa's heart. There was no getting around it. He might as well get it over with.

Jeremy Aames

<u>Things</u> <u>to</u> <u>do:</u>

Mow the lawn
Pay the water bill
Cancel the cable
Dishes
Call Ally about working more hours
Chemistry lab
Research for history report
Finish <u>Portrait</u> <u>of</u> <u>the</u> <u>Artist</u> <u>as</u> <u>a</u> <u>Young</u> <u>Man</u>
Call Trent
~~Get Jessica's phone number from Liz~~
Buy newspaper and give Dad the Classified section
Coupons
Get Jessica's number from Liz

CHAPTER

Giving Up

12

"I can't believe you guys did that," Maria said, rifling through the cosmetic bottles next to the sink. "No means no by the pool too."

"I know," Andy said. "Liz, I'm so sorry. We were just messing around."

Elizabeth sighed and stared at her drowned-rat reflection. "It's okay, Andy. I'll live." *I'm just never going to be able to look Conner in the face again,* she thought.

"Do you want me to get you a T-shirt or something?" Andy asked.

"Yeah, thanks," Elizabeth said. She was still wrapped in the towel, and she didn't want to go back outside for her clothes at the moment.

"I'll be right back," Andy said.

"I'm such a moron," Elizabeth said, covering her face with her hands. She pictured herself emerging from the pool—her hair stuck to her face and these huge black rings around her eyes. She even had black drips running down her cheeks.

"It wasn't that bad," Maria said. She saturated a cotton ball with makeup remover and handed it to Elizabeth. "Since when did you start wearing so much makeup anyway?"

"I was just trying it out," Elizabeth said, going to work on her face. "Trial period over. The package said it was waterproof."

"Yeah. In a slight drizzle, maybe," Maria said.

Andy appeared at the door. "Here you go." He handed Elizabeth an orange El Carro High T-shirt.

"Thanks," Elizabeth said. She pulled the soft cotton shirt over her head and checked her reflection. She looked better, but not great. Orange wasn't exactly her color, and the stupid zit on her chin was all throbbing and red now. Somehow she didn't feel like partying anymore.

"I think I'm just gonna go," she said, tossing the blackened cotton ball in the trash can.

"Oh, come on. Don't leave," Andy begged. "Evan and I will die of guilt."

"Good," Elizabeth joked halfheartedly. "Seriously, though. I'm just tired, and I don't feel like going back out there." She paused and pulled the rubber band out of her hair. "Maria, do you think you could get my bag?"

"Sure," Maria said. "Just wait here."

Andy pushed his hands through his unruly red curls. "I'll go tell Evan we have to sit around and mope for the rest of the day," he said with a small smile.

164

"Don't worry about it, really," Elizabeth asserted.

"I'll call you later," Andy said. He started off down the hall. "Scaring people away from my own party," he muttered.

Elizabeth smirked. She shook her head as she pulled a brush through her wet hair. It was time to admit defeat. Conner might have noticed her for five seconds, but she'd made an idiot of herself one too many times for him to ever really be interested.

The kiss wasn't going to happen. It was time for Elizabeth to just accept it.

Will was starting to worry. Not that anything could have happened to Melissa between the field and the parking lot, but maybe she'd already left. Maybe she was blowing him off to get back at him for ditching her. He couldn't take waiting around much longer.

He checked out the parking lot and noticed that both Cherie and Lila's cars were there. Were they all still inside? Maybe they were planning another anti-Jessica campaign. If so, he was going to run some interference on this one.

Will locked the door of his truck and walked up to the school. The place was eerily quiet, but he could hear muffled voices coming from inside the auxiliary gym. Will tiptoed over to the door and peeked inside. Melissa was sitting in the middle of the beat-up, black wrestling mat that covered the gym floor, surrounded by Gina, Amy, Cherie, and Lila. Melissa was bent over at the waist, crying.

He almost turned around and walked out, but Cherie looked up and spotted him hovering. "Hey, Will," she said with a sad, resigned look on her face. "Come on in."

Will inched into the room. He knew everyone expected him to throw his arms around Melissa and ask her what was wrong, but he was tired of it. He was tired of the fact that she was always crying or always looking over her shoulder. It was taking too much out of him, and he wasn't even sure she was genuinely upset half the time.

Melissa looked up, and her face was soaked. "Will," she said with a sniffle. "Tia told on us."

"What?" Will asked.

"I didn't make captain," Melissa continued. She made no move to get up, and he made no move to go to her. "Tia did."

Will was floored. Tia Ramirez made captain? That was out of left field. But he didn't get the connection between that and the tattling thing.

"I'm sorry, Liss." He walked over and sat down in front of her, his legs crossed Indian style. "I really am. But how do you know she told on you?"

"Think about it," Cherie said. "She and Jessica went in there and told Laufeld the whole story and made themselves look all rosy. It's so obvious."

Oh. So apparently they thought Jessica was in on it too. Why was he not surprised?

"I don't know," Will said. "It doesn't add up."

"What do you mean, it doesn't add up?" Melissa asked, sobbing. "This is all Jessica's fault. First she tries to steal you. Then she talks about me to everyone right in front of me. And the one time I try to fight back, she bad-mouths me to the coach. She's trying to take everything away from me."

Melissa's voice broke, and she sobbed quietly into her hands. Will's guilt weighed down on him like a lead jacket. He'd done this to Melissa. He'd cheated on her and turned her into this paranoid person capable of taking revenge and twisting the truth.

Will moved over to sit next to Melissa, and Lila slid out of the way. When he put his arms around her, she collapsed onto his chest. Will didn't believe that Jessica would tell on Melissa. It just wasn't in her. She wouldn't slam someone else to get her way. And if Tia *had* told, she would have only been telling the truth. Melissa had behaved horribly. But he couldn't tell his girlfriend that.

"I'm right here," Will said as he stroked her hair back from her face. "I'm not gonna leave."

He couldn't ever leave her after what he'd done to her—after what he'd done with Jessica.

Jessica kicked a broken paper cup in front of her as she walked down the sidewalk on Main Street.

167

Her chin was tucked and she was staring at the ground, trying to avoid the curious glances of Saturday-afternoon shoppers. She knew they were all wondering why a girl was walking around downtown in a cheerleading uniform, carrying her pompoms, and looking totally morose.

I should have gone back, Jessica thought. *I can't believe I skipped a game.* She was definitely off the team now. There was no way she could explain her behavior today. She couldn't even explain it to herself. All she knew was that she didn't want to face Melissa's smug expression. She didn't want to hear what her teammates had said to Jeremy, and she knew they would have found a way of letting her know.

The sun was beating down on Jessica's back, and she suddenly felt very tired. She'd told her mom she would call her when she was ready to come home, but she had no idea what time it was. Would the game be over yet? Jessica looked around for someone to ask for the time. That was when she realized she was standing across the street from House of Java.

She just stood there and stared, remembering her breakfast with Jeremy. Had that really been this morning? Everything had changed in only a few hours. Now Jeremy knew she was an outcast— a social leper. A slut. Jessica plopped down on a bench, feeling exhausted.

Cherie had probably asked him point-blank why he was talking to such a loser. Then after a bit of confusion on Jeremy's part, they would have warned him away from Jessica—told him she was a boyfriend-stealing back stabber and he should stay away. Jessica knew they weren't above it. They'd already done much worse.

Jessica blinked back tears. She just wanted to go home. Not back to Lila's house, but home. To her bed, her room, her parents, her sister.

For two short days House of Java had been a place to escape to, but now it was over.

Jessica sighed and peeled her eyes from House of Java. She knew she should call her mother and ask her to come pick her up, but that would mean going back to the mansion and seeing Lila, who would probably say something about her missing the game in front of her parents. Then she'd have to explain that.

"Maybe Elizabeth is home," she said, her hopes starting to rise. She could hang out with Elizabeth over at the Sandborns'. No one there had anything against her . . . as far as she knew.

Jessica found a pay phone and dialed Elizabeth's new number. The phone picked up on the third ring.

"Hello?"

"Mrs. Sandborn? This is Jessica Wakefield," she said.

"Elizabeth?"

Jessica smiled. "No, Jessica. Elizabeth is my sister. Is she there?"

"Oh, well, no, dear," Mrs. Sandborn said, sounding confused. "She's at a party. She's been at a party all day."

Jessica's heart dropped. All day? As in, not at Healthy? "Are you sure?" Jessica asked. "I thought she was working this afternoon."

Mrs. Sandborn laughed. "Only if she was going to work in a bikini."

"A bikini?" Jessica repeated. She was thoroughly confused. "Elizabeth doesn't wear bikinis."

"Well, she did today." Mrs. Sandborn sighed, sounding impatient. "Should I leave her a message?"

"No, thanks," Jessica said quickly. She hung up the phone, feeling her knees grow weak. Was it possible? Had Elizabeth actually missed Jessica's shift to go to a party? Her manager would never stand for that. He was an ex-hippie, but he ran the store as if he'd been in the military.

"No," Jessica said aloud. "This is Elizabeth we're talking about." She managed a small laugh. "She'd probably burst into flames if she was that irresponsible."

Of course, there was one sure way to find out. Healthy was only a few blocks away, toward the center of town. And it wasn't like Jessica had anything better to do.

Her heart pounded as she made her way along the sidewalk. What if Elizabeth hadn't shown up? How would she explain that to Jim? Jessica sighed and tried to calm her nerves. This was stupid. There was no way Elizabeth had bailed.

Jessica turned and walked into the health-food store. The place was practically deserted. Beach was behind the counter. His back was to her, but there was no mistaking the long, blond ponytail and deeply tanned skin. He turned around when he heard her walk in.

"Hey, Beach," Jessica said.

He started to smile, but then his face fell. "Where have you *been?*" he hissed. He looked over his shoulder toward Jim's office.

Jessica's stomach hit the tiled floor.

Beach looked down at her outfit. "Did you have a game?"

"I—well, yeah." Jessica had no idea what to say.

"You should have told Jim," Beach said, leaning over the green Formica countertop. "Or at least called in sick," he added.

"I . . . I know," Jessica stammered. "I totally spaced on my shift."

"Well, maybe you should get out of here," Beach whispered. "If he doesn't see you in that costume, then maybe you can tell him you were . . . I don't know, kidnapped by aliens or something."

"Is he in a bad mood?" Jessica asked. Her knees were quivering.

Beach rolled his eyes. "That's an understatement. He got an entire shipment of bad kiwi, and they won't take it back."

171

Just then the office door flew open and Jim stormed out. He paused when he saw Jessica. "Decided to grace us with your presence?" he asked, slapping a stack of papers onto the counter. His face was all red, and the tufts of gray hair above his ears were sticking straight out.

"I'm really sorry—," Jessica began.

"You know what? I don't care," Jim said. He was flipping through the papers, but he wasn't even looking at them. "You don't show up. You don't call. You're outta here. There are plenty of people around here who *need* this job." His eyes roamed over her outfit. "And would take it seriously."

"I do take it seriously," Jessica protested. "Please just let me explain."

Jim ran a hand over his balding head. "You can pick up your last paycheck next week," he said. With that he turned, stalked back to his office, and slammed the door.

"Ouch," Beach said, wincing. "You want me to talk to him after he calms down?"

"No," Jessica said numbly. "Yeah. I don't know."

She turned away from Beach so he wouldn't see the tears flooding her eyes. *Elizabeth,* she thought, *where are you?*

"That's the last party I go to for a long time," Elizabeth muttered to herself as she popped open the door of the Jeep. She threw her bag onto the passenger seat and pulled down on the back of Andy's oversized T-shirt. She hadn't put on her shorts because she didn't want to get them wet, and she wanted to cover her butt so she wouldn't make the seat wet too. She climbed into the car and leaned back her head.

"What a weird day," she said with a sigh. At that moment Conner walked out the end of the driveway and over to his car. Just as he was unlocking the door, he looked up and spotted her. He started to walk over. "And about to get weirder," Elizabeth added under her breath.

Conner had pulled on a white T-shirt over his baggy blue bathing suit. He was all freshly tan, and his hair glistened as if he'd just gotten out of the pool. He looked incredible.

"You're leaving?" he asked. Elizabeth couldn't believe he'd come to talk to her. Now. When she was wet and makeupless and sitting here in a loud orange shirt with no pants on.

"Yeah. I think I've provided enough entertainment for one day."

Conner smirked. "It wasn't that bad."

"Did you just say something to make me feel better?" Elizabeth asked incredulously. She grabbed her bag and started digging through it for a pad. "Wait a minute. I have to write this down."

"Mark the time," Conner said. He started to walk away, and Elizabeth tried to think of something to make him stay. Then he walked around her car and climbed into the now empty passenger seat.

Elizabeth pulled out her keys and tossed her bag into the backseat. "Did you want a ride?" she asked, trying to figure out what he was doing.

"I have a car," he said. Conner looked up at the clear, blue sky. "Must be nice at night."

"What?" Elizabeth asked. "Oh! The car. But you have a convertible."

"Top's busted." Conner cocked his head out the window and adjusted the side mirror. "It won't go down."

"Oh," Elizabeth said. They sat in silence for a few moments, and Elizabeth was conscious of how her last words hung in the air. She tugged at the hem of the T-shirt and shifted in her seat.

"Can I ask you something?" Conner said suddenly.

Elizabeth was surprised at the hint of uncertainty in his voice. This time he wasn't about to mock her. He glanced at her and then faced forward again.

"It's about Maria," he said.

Oh, no, Elizabeth thought. *He wants her back. He's going to ask me how to get her back.*

"Is she okay?" he asked. "I mean, she's not, like, devastated or anything?"

"Devastated?" Elizabeth repeated.

"I know. I know. It sounds egotistical, right?" he asked. "She's just been acting weird lately, you know? Always hanging around . . ."

"And you don't want her hanging around," Elizabeth stated.

"No. It's not that." Conner let out an exasperated sigh. "I just don't want her to get the wrong idea," he said.

"Maria's a good person," Elizabeth said. "You really hurt her."

Conner paused and looked out the side of the car. "I know."

Elizabeth was confused. "Is there something you want me to tell her, or . . ."

"No. Forget it," Conner said. He glanced at her and semismiled. "I guess the sun is affecting my brain."

"Maybe we should go," Elizabeth said, lifting her keys out of her lap.

"Yeah." Conner started to open his door, and Elizabeth's keys slipped out of her hand. They hit the center console and slipped down next to Conner's seat.

"I got it," Conner said.

Elizabeth's hand was already searching the space when Conner leaned over to help. His cheek brushed hers, and Elizabeth froze. Her face stung where his stubble had brushed her skin. She was about to spring back, but Conner wasn't moving.

She could feel his breath on her neck, just behind her ear. She could smell the chlorine in his hair.

Slowly Conner started to pull away. Elizabeth still couldn't move. She was looking into his eyes. He was staring at her—staring into her, through her.

This is it, Elizabeth thought.

And then he kissed her. His lips touched hers softly. Very softly. And Elizabeth started to float. She was leaving the earth behind. She could feel Conner's kiss in every inch of her body. It was the sweetest touch she'd ever experienced.

And in a moment, it was over.

Conner jerked away and pressed himself back into his seat. Elizabeth's heart was pounding in her ears, but she still could have sworn she heard him utter the word *damn.*

Elizabeth sat up. "Conner—"

"I have to go." He was out of the car in seconds.

"Okay," she said quietly.

He paused outside, as if the Jeep's half door was enough of a barrier to make him feel safe. "I'll ... I'll see you at home," he said. Then he walked down the street to his car.

Elizabeth's hands were shaking as she fumbled around for her keys. She finally found them and started the car just as Conner's Mustang roared by. Elizabeth sat for a few more moments, trying to regain her sanity. But one thought kept repeating itself in her mind.

Tia was right. You could tell everything from one kiss.

JESSICA WAKEFIELD
5:35 P.M.

I'm fired. Elizabeth didn't show. She didn't call in. She didn't even call _me_ and leave a message. And now I'm fired. Beach called me and said Jim wouldn't even talk to _him_ about it.

So let's add it up.

I have no house.

I have no friends.

I have no boyfriend.

I have no cheerleading squad.

I have no job.

And I have one, soon-to-be-deceased, sister.

I have no life.

ELIZABETH WAKEFIELD
5:36 P.M.

Do you know what I just realized?
He kissed me.
Ha!

CONNER MCDERMOTT
5:36 P.M.

I kissed her.

What's wrong with me?

I usually know exactly what I'm doing, exactly why I'm doing it, and exactly what the fallout is gonna be. And I'm usually prepared for it.

Not this time. This time . . . I'm drawing a blank.

JEREMY AAMES
5:45 P.M.

So what if the house falls down around us and I maybe, possibly, get my heart slammed?

Dad thinks I should be dating. And I'm a good guy. I listen to my parents. So I think that's what I'm gonna do. I'm gonna date.

I just hope Jessica is willing to cooperate.

Check out the **all-new....**

Sweet Valley Web site—

www.sweetvalley.com

New Features

Cool Prizes

The
ONLY
official
Web site!

Hot Links

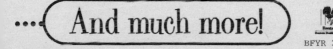

And much more!

Bantam
Doubleday Dell
BFYR 202

The *ONLY* Official Book on Today's Hottest Band!

Over 80 EXCLUSIVE color photos!

0-440-41636-1

Get up close and personal with Justin, J.C., Lance, Chris, and Joey as they discuss—in their own words—their music, their friendships on and offstage, their fans, and much more!

On sale now wherever books are sold.

And don't miss

Available wherever music and videos are sold.

www.nsync.com

Dell
BFYR 215A

Francine Pascal's SVH **senioryear**

You're watching
"Dawson's Creek"...

You're wearing
Urban Decay...

Have you read
senioryear?

Bantam

www.sweetvalley.com

BFYR 232